Shine

When Kate Maryon isn't writing, or walking her large Newfoundland dog, Ellie, or spending time with her grown up children, Jane and Tim, or her grown-up stepchildren, Sam, Joe and Ben, or having fun with her husband Daniel, or visiting the rest of her family, or sitting in cafés and other lovely places with her friends, she can be found working from a clinic in Somerset, where she practises homeopathy, or in Devon where she works on detox retreats. And with all this going on there's never a shortage of stories and wonderful things to write about.

Kate loves chocolate, films, eating out, reading, writing and lying on sunny beaches. She dislikes snakes, spiders, peppermint and honey.

Also by Kate Maryon

Glitter

A Million Angels

Shine

Kate Maryon x

HarperCollins *Children's Books*

First published in Great Britain by HarperCollins *Children's Books* 2010
This edition published in 2011
HarperCollins *Children's Books* is a division of HarperCollins*Publishers* Ltd,
77-85 Fulham Palace Road, Hammersmith, London W6 8JB

The HarperCollins *Children's Books* website address is
www.harpercollins.co.uk

4

Shine
Text copyright © Kate Maryon 2010

ISBN-13 978-0-00-7433179

Typeset in AGaramond by Palimpsest Book Production Limited,
Falkirk, Stirlingshire

For my brother Tim and sister Susie,
Against all odds, like stars at night we shine.
I love you both with all my heart x

Chapter 1

She's just like a real magpie...

My mum totally loves shiny things, like silver and gold and jewels and big, fast, shiny cars. Mikey, her business partner, calls her 'Magpie' because she's always on the lookout for things, just like one of those magpie-birds that takes shiny stuff and hoards it in its nest. The only difference is that my mum hoards things in our flat, which means if she doesn't stop soon we'll be facing an emergency situation due to lack of space.

The thing I worry about most is that my mum says she can't stop herself. She is truly addicted. And the worst thing is that often she doesn't even buy things, she just takes them. Anything shiny is just too tempting for her. Some people might call it 'stealing'; my mum calls it 'borrowing'. It *is* stealing though and, well, that's not exactly a good thing is it? And though me and Mum do some pretty cool stuff, sometimes she can be so embarrassing. Like the other day when we were walking through the market and she saw a fluffy scarf that she wanted for me. She just strolled up to the stall and while she was busy talking to the lady about the weather, she slipped it into her bag. And then what am I supposed to do? I can hardly scream "Thief" and get my mum arrested for shoplifting! So I just stay close and keep my mouth shut, and if people notice we make a run for it, fast.

I also know that she spends money on the internet using other people's credit cards. You might think that's a good thing for me because I have stuff, like three iPods, seven watches, a drawer full of rings, bangles and necklaces, two giant plasma TVs and my own laptop. And I do like getting all that stuff. . . and I love my mum and we're a team, just me and her. But sometimes I wish she was more like a normal mum. I can't tell anyone the truth about the stealing or say anything to her about it because I don't want to upset her, and I'm afraid that if I do say anything she'll go off on one of her temper tantrums, which means she'll go straight out to the shops again, just to cheer herself up.

Last month we had a row and Mum drank loads of wine. Then she went out and came back with an amazing mega-red sports car that Mikey got hold of. I wanted us to make up, so I squashed down my worries and had fun as Mum and me zoomed about all over the place with the roof down wearing headscarves and big sunglasses like movie stars do. "Living the dream, that's what we're doing, babe," Mum giggled as we raced down the High Street. But a couple of days ago Mum got bored of it, and sold it on to this uber-rich lady while I was at school.

"We've done it, babe, the world's our oyster!" she squealed, as she showed me the hugest mountain of cash I've ever seen. We danced around the living room like crazy things, throwing our money-confetti high up in the air and letting it fall down on us like paper rain.

Right then we knew that the money would change our days. But we didn't know how much it would change our lives.

Chapter 2

A woman possessed by the idea of a dog...

After school the next day we get down to business, writing big, fat shopping lists and making plans. I am determined not to think about where the money came from and I'm trying to join in with the fun. I find a sheet of plain paper and a marker pen and draw a line down the middle. I write "Tiff" at the top of one column and "Carla", that's my mum's name, at the top of the other. In Mum's column I write the things she wants: 1) new perfume 2) some more diamond earrings 3) a pair of boots with shiny buckles 4) champagne. Under my name I write: 1) pencil case 2) new tops 3) a book and 4) a pet.

"Don't even go there, Tiff," says Mum, "There's just no way, not ever, that I could put up with a pooping, piddling pet scatting about the house."

"A pony?" I ask, hopefully. "A pony wouldn't even come near the house."

Mum raises her eyebrows and slurps her glass of wine. I can see that something is on her mind.

"My dad got me and Cass ponies when we moved to Sark. . . mine was called Mabel and. . . Oh, never mind, Tiff," she sighs. "The answer's no and that's that. Can we not go on about it any more, please? You're giving me a headache."

And I know not to go on, or ask any more questions, because my mum *never* talks about her past. Except occasionally, when she's had too much wine to drink and the words sort of slip out of her mouth. But once she realises what she's doing she *always* stops herself and changes the subject, especially when the subject happens to be Sark, the tiny island her family moved to when she was little. All I know is that my mum ran away from Sark when she was seventeen and has never been back since. I've never been, full stop. And I've never even met or seen a photo of my dad because he ran off before I was born. And I don't know her family, including my grandparents and my Auntie Cass.

"In the bright lights, babe, that's where we belong." Mum always says. So we never talk about anything old. In our life everything's always shiny and new.

She takes a brush to my hair and tugs at my tangles. She takes another glug of wine. "Come on, cheer up," she says, kissing me on the end of my nose. "Let's have some fun shopping and then we can grab us one of our super-famous slap-up dinners. How would that be?"

"OK," I say, "but no funny stuff, promise?"

"Promise," she winks, drawing two big red lines of lipstick across her lips and smacking them together. "You know me, Tiff. It's you and me," she says.

"You and me, Mum," I echo, switching off the TV.

After a bit of retail therapy, where my mum actually managed to keep her fingers to herself and pay for our treats with cash, she decides we need go to Miguel's to have our hair and nails done. I *really, really* want to have my hair cut all short and choppy, but Mum insists I keep it long. She loves the way she can brush it and make it all smooth and shiny.

"But I want a proper hairstyle! I'm twelve, Mum; I'm not a little girl. And Chelsea's having hers done!"

"I said no, Tiff, and that is the end of the haircut conversation."

And, just like always, Mum gets her way and I have to go along with it.

"Coooooeeeee, Carla," shrieks Bianca, my mum's best friend, when we walk into Miguel's place. She starts leaping up and down in the chair and waving her arms about like a wild thing. "Come and look over here!"

We go over to where she's sipping coffee and having more highlights put in her ice-blonde hair. My mum and Bianca hug like mad things and jump up and down like they haven't seen each other for at least a hundred years. Bianca grabs my cheeks and squeezes them hard in a friendly kind of a way.

"Ooh, you two are gonna be so jealous when I show you what I have in here," she squeals, pointing at her bag. "Look what Harry got me. Can you believe it?"

I do look, and a little pink puppy nose peeps over the top of the bag, and a tiny ball of white fluff wags its tail. Bianca lifts 'Queenie' out of the bag and puts her on the floor, and everyone in Miguel's – especially me – goes crazy for her until she does a little tiddle on Miguel's gleaming white tiles. Then Miguel starts huffing about the place saying it's a salon he's running here, not a zoo.

Mum changes her mind about having our slap-up meal because we spent so long having our hair and nails done. But I don't mind because when we're on our way home she starts talking and I totally can't believe what my ears are hearing.

"I just *have* to have one!" Mum's wailing like a three-year-old. "I *really, really, really* have to have one."

It was only a few hours ago my mum totally refused to even consider the idea of having a pet. But now that her best friend has a puppy, suddenly everything has changed. She is *so* childish! But right now, I'm trying to think of the positives, and I'm totally fizzing inside with excitement. I don't want to say anything at all that will make her change her mind because I know we'll be getting our own puppy uber-quick-pronto. You see words like *wait, patience* and *think* just aren't in her brain dictionary. She loves things to be fast, like fast cars and fast food.

"OK, so let's go to the rescue place," I suggest.

"Good idea," she says, "for *some* people. But not for us, Tiff! The whole rescue-dog thing would take too long to sort out. I've made up my mind: I want a dog and I want it now."

"Muuumm," I say, worrying that she's up to no good, "what are you planning?"

"Don't panic, babe, even *I* wouldn't take someone's dog! And anyway, we don't want a boring old biffer of a dog, do we? We want something new; something special."

I try to argue that rescue-dogs need good homes, but as usual Mum gets her way. We have bags and bags of cash to splash so we head off to the place where Bianca got Queenie and hand over £800 for a cute little white fluff-a-fluff. I fall in love with her straightaway.

"Let's call her Powder Puff," I say, trying to think of a good name, "or Snowflake."

"Good try, Tiff, but I really can't see myself standing in the park every morning shouting out 'Powder Puff, Powder Puff', can you? And she's really not a frosty little snowflake is she?"

I have a feeling it doesn't really matter what I think

in this situation. Mum goes to the fridge, throws me a Coke and pours herself a glass of her favourite white wine, Chardonnay.

"I've got it!" she shrieks. "She's a *Chardonnay* from head to tail! Don't you just love it, babe?"

And I suppose I do. So we get out my favourite hairbrush and give Chardonnay her first proper pamper session. Then we get busy on the internet ordering things that we think a puppy might need. We choose a shiny diamanté collar, a pink lead, some pink polka-dot dog bowls and a proper princess-bed with a special silk doggy duvet. We go crazy over dog clothes and order Chardonnay a tartan outfit and hat for rainy days, a pink party dress for celebration days and a little pink tracksuit for everyday park-wear.

Just when we're about to order ourselves a takeaway, Mum's mobile springs into life and blares out a show tune.

"Mikey-babe," she says. Then she's listening for a while and I notice that she's nibbling her brand-new nails. "Right, OK, see you there then."

She dumps Chardonnay on my lap. "Sorry, Tiff, I just have to go and meet Mikey for a bit. I'll be back soon. You all right with Chardonnay?"

"Sure," I say, my tummy rumbling. "See you later alligator."

"In a while crocodile. And, babe," she says, halfway out of the door, "I've been thinking that we deserve a holiday. Monte Carlo, Las Vegas, Hawaii, wherever you fancy."

The amazing holiday we had last year flashes into my mind. We went to Barbados and stayed in this uber-cool hotel and pretended we were real princesses. We just had to click our fingers and we got whatever we wanted.

"Barbados again?" I say.

"Hm. I was thinking of somewhere new," says Mum. "Let's check out the brochures tomorrow. And, hey, why don't you call Chelsea and get her to come round for a sleepover, to keep you company?"

"Brilliant idea, Mum," I say. "Thanks."

She comes over and kisses me on the top of my head.

"You have to look after your friends, Tiff, make them feel special." She's twiddling one of my blonde waves round and round her finger and I catch on her face that far-away look, that thinking-of-her-old-life look.

"The thing is, Tiff," she continues, "you never know

what's going to happen in life. One day you might wake up to discover that your friends have gone, that they just aren't there for you any more. So take my advice, babe, and treasure them while you can."

It's kind of weird for my mum to say stuff like that, and I'm sure I see a tiny tear escape from the corner of her eye. She wipes it away and heads for the door again. "You and me, babe," she calls through a perfume haze.

Chapter 3

Craaaaaaazy about Tiffany's...

When it's just Chardonnay and me I call my best friend, Chelsea, to see if she can come over. She only lives in the same block of flats as us, but her dad's quite a worry guts, so ten minutes later, when she gets dropped off, I pretend that my mum's just popped out to buy some milk.

"What shall we do, Tiff?" asks Chelsea, plaiting Chardonnay's fringe.

"Definitely an old movie," I say. "*Wizard of Oz*?"

"Why, of course," says Chelsea, in the American voice we sometimes use when we're playing around. Then we move into action. First we pile the sofa high with cushions and duvets and put out loads of snacks in tiny bowls. Then we get all dressed up in two of Mum's glittery dresses and put on our sparkly high-heeled ruby slippers that we bought for each other last Christmas. We put on loads of Mum's make-up, tie up our hair and make two delicious Shirley Temple cocktails.

"Your mum's so cool, Tiff," says Chelsea. "Mine would go crazy if I even went anywhere *near* her make-up. If I used it, I think she'd just totally explode. And she'd never leave me in the house alone. My parents still think I'm about five years old, or something, and they act like they're at least a hundred."

"Mum likes me using her stuff," I say. "We share everything. She trusts me and I trust her." My voice wobbles a bit when I hear myself talking to Chels about trust. Because I think that my mum does trust me, but I'm not so sure that I completely trust her. "Come on," I say, changing the subject, "let's watch the movie."

Chelsea and I love all the old-fashioned films. Things like the original *Parent Trap* and *Whistle Down the Wind* and *Pollyanna* with Hayley Mills in them. They're so much better than new ones. *The Wizard of Oz* is our all-time favourite, with Judy Garland playing Dorothy.

Breakfast at Tiffany's is my mum's favourite and it's where she got my name from. Tiffany's is this amazing, expensive jewellery shop in New York, and there's one in London too, and it was the first place Mum wanted to go to when she ran away from Sark.

Chels and I know all the words from all the movies off by heart because we've watched them so many times. And sometimes we even turn the sound right down and do the voice bits ourselves.

"*Toto*," I say to Chelsea, messing about in my best American accent, handing her some Pringles, "*I've a feeling we're not in Kansas any more.*"

"*I know*," says Chels, giggling, "*we must be over the rainbow.*"

And then we just get the giggles and snorts big-time and turn off all the lights and snuggle down with Chardonnay to watch.

"What now?" asks Chels when the film has finished and we're giving each other a proper face-mask pamper-treatment.

"How about a horror movie?" I say. "Something really spoooooky. Let's see what's on." I start surfing through the channels. There's loads of boring stuff on and just as we are about to give up I see Mikey's face splashed all over *Crimewatch*. My heart drops into my tummy and starts churning around like a washing machine on full spin. This isn't the kind of horror thing I was looking for.

"Er, Tiff," says Chelsea. "Isn't that your mum's friend? And look, there's that big red sports car that you and your mum had last week."

I realise that I'm just sitting there staring at the screen. My mouth has turned into the Sahara Desert and my voice has done a runner. I stare and stare at Mikey's face on the TV. It's one of those police photos that makes him look all scary, like a murderer. I don't want to watch, but my hands can't make the remote work.

"Looks like he's in big trouble," says Chels, edging closer to the screen.

My chest has heavy birds flapping inside, and someone's fist is in my tummy, squeezing it tight. I don't really know what's happening, but I know that something is *very, very, very* wrong. My hands are shaking and I spill lemonade all over the place while I make us more drinks.

The doorbell rings. I open it and Chelsea's dad is standing there with a boiling-mad face.

"Where's your mum, Tiff?" he gruffs.

I can't speak.

"Grab your things, Chels," he says, "you're coming home with me."

"But I'm sleeping over, Dad," she argues, still covered in my mum's expensive face cream.

"It's not up for discussion, Chelsea," he says. "You're coming home now and that's that. And *you*," he says, staring goggle-eyed at me, "you tell your mum it's not right to leave under-fourteens on their own in the house. Tell her it's downright dangerous, got it?"

I nod, trying to keep control of my bottom lip. It's gone all stupid and keeps twitching and trembling. Chelsea takes off Mum's dress, pulls on her jeans and shoves her ruby slippers and sleepover stuff in her bag.

"You gonna be OK, Tiff?" she asks, squeezing my hand.

I squeeze her hand back and paint on a smile, then the door slams and I'm left alone with Chardonnay, wondering. My whole body follows my lip and turns to jelly. I'm freezing and shaking. I close the curtains and double-lock the door. Then I switch channels to a comedy thing, hide under the duvet with Chardonnay, and wait.

Chapter 4

You're such a little worry guts. . .

"Quick, Tiff!" Mum calls out, slamming the front door, "We're going on that holiday. Now! Get your bits together, babe, you know: sun cream, bikini, iPod, that new book you bought."

She stumbles into the flat and trips over Chardonnay, who's wagging her tail and panting like crazy, pleased to see Mum. I'm pleased to see her too, and my jelly body melts a bit and calms down. I don't feel so scared now she's home.

"I saw Mikey," I say. "I saw Mikey on the telly. His face was all over *Crimewatch* and Chelsea saw everything and then her dad came and got all cross that you weren't here and took her home."

"What you talking about, Tiff?" she says, pulling our wheelie bags from the cupboard in the hall. "Mikey's not on telly, he's been with me, babe. You must've got it wrong."

"But Mum," I persist, rescuing Chardonnay from her spiky heels, "I saw him, and there was a picture of that red car we had, and I need you to tell me what's going on." The washing machine starts up in my tummy again and the birds begin flapping in my brain.

"Oh, Tiff, lighten up," she says, in a harsh voice. "You're such a little worry guts. Trust me, baby, trust me."

I stare cold eyes at her.

"You do trust me, Tiff, don't you? I couldn't bear it if you didn't."

And then her eyes start welling up, and I can't make her cry so I put a cheerful face on to calm her down, but my worries keep on nibbling at my brain.

"Why are we going *now*?" I ask. "I thought we were going to look at the brochures tomorrow and choose somewhere together. And there's a new rule at school and we have to get special permission to go away during term-time. We have to wait till Monday, Mum. Please? And let them know properly."

"Worry guts," Mum teases, rushing about the place with her bikini in her hand. "We're going on holiday now because Mikey managed to get a special deal. Don't you worry your pretty little head about boring old school, I've got it all under control. Come on now, we've got to hurry, babe, he'll be here for us any minute now."

I ignore our dressing-up mess and try to squeeze myself into the holiday mood. But I don't feel very holidayish. I feel more worried, and I hate not knowing what's really going on. I squash my worries down because now isn't the time to set my mum off on one of her moods. When your mum has big tantrums like mine does, you get very good at learning how to squash your own feelings down so she doesn't go crazy.

"Where are we going, Mum?" I ask, trying hard to sound chirpy and excited. "Is it somewhere we can have cocktails and mocktails on the balcony? Like last year?"

We're both busy stuffing clothes and last summer's sandals into our bags.

"Not sure, yet, babe," she says, getting our passports from the drawer. "We'll have a real adventure this time, you know, like in the movies. We thought we'd hop on a ferry from Dover to France and just keep on driving towards the sun."

She's talking really fast and her voice sounds all squeaky and high and her hands are trembling. Just then a car horn blares away in the street outside.

"Time to go," says Mum. Then she starts swaying about and singing, "We're all going on an – autumn holiday; no more working for a week or two." And I know that she wants me to join in with her, and I try, but the words somehow get stuck in the little worry bag that's sitting in my throat.

We turn off the lights and head for the door.

"What about Chardonnay?" I ask.

"Oh, worry guts again. Chardonnay'll be all right, Tiff. We'll ring Bianca – she'll look after her. Come on, Mikey's waiting."

But I don't budge.

"I'm not leaving her," I say. "She's just a tiny puppy that you were completely crazy about getting only this afternoon, Mum. If you hadn't noticed, she can't take care of herself. And she's ours, not Bianca's. She'd be scared on her own – it's cruel."

"Tiff, I'm telling you, it's time to go. Now is not the time for questions."

"No, Mum," I say. "What's happening? This whole holiday thing doesn't feel right. It's too sudden. We never just pack our bags and go. And I *did* see Mikey on *Crimewatch* and Chelsea saw it too. It's not in my imagination, it's real, Mum. And it's not normal to just pack your bags in the middle of the night and go on holiday. So if Chardonnay's staying, then I'm staying too."

Mum switches the lights back on and stares me out.

"I said it's time to go, Tiff."

"And I said I'm not leaving without Chardonnay."

I'm good at staring people out. Chelsea and I practise it all the time and see who can last the longest. After a while my mum huffs, makes her way to the kitchen and takes a slug from a half-finished bottle of wine.

"You win," she says, "but stuff her in your bag and keep her quiet for a bit. Mikey'll murder me when he finds out."

The car horn down in the street blasts out again. I grab a couple of tins of puppy food and a bottle of water and follow Mum out.

"You excited, honey?" she slurs, swigging on her wine, while we're standing in the lift. "I think you're too much of a worry guts for your age, Tiff. You shouldn't be worried about life when you're twelve years old. I bet Chelsea would jump at the chance of having this kind of adventure. It's fun going away on a surprise holiday. You remember that word, Tiff, you know, the *fun, fun, fun* word? Ah, I do love you though," she breathes wine breath in my ear and kisses my cheek. "My little star. You and me, babe," she says. "You and me."

I turn away from her, still angry, but tired of arguing and sad that she's drunk again. I busy myself with making a safe, cosy nest in my rucksack for Chardonnay, and I zip her in so Mikey won't see.

Chapter 5

There'll be bluebells over, the white cliffs of Dover...

Mikey's waiting for us in a car I've never seen before. We throw our stuff in the boot and climb in. Mikey's puffing away on a fat cigar. Mum shares her wine with him and off we roar, away from London, away from home.

"You excited, Tiffany?" asks Mikey, puffing thick cigar smoke all around the car. "Who knows where we're going to end up, eh? Ooh, somewhere hot for me, please."

I force a smile, do up my seat belt and peer at Chardonnay. Luckily she's already snoozing away in her cosy rucksack nest. Mum and Mikey start droning on about boring stuff and making rude jokes. It's dark and late and the car is full of smoke, but I know Mikey's face and I know I saw it on *Crimewatch*. I guess I must have fallen asleep because the next thing I know is that Mum is shaking me awake.

"Wakey, wakey, sleepyhead," she's saying, "wakey, wakey."

I open my eyes. It's really dark outside and raining hard. I stuff my hand in my rucksack and give Chardonnay a reassuring stroke. She licks my fingers and snuggles back down. My neck aches from sleeping in the car and I badly need a wee from all the Shirley Temples that Chels and I had drunk. This doesn't feel like a fun holiday to me, but Mum and Mikey are laughing and having a good time.

"We're in Dover, Tiff," says Mum, then she and Mikey start singing some old song, "*There'll be bluebells over, the white cliffs of Dover . . .*"

We pull up in the line of cars queuing to get on the ferry. Mikey's holding all our passports and he keeps tap, tap, tapping them on the steering wheel, waiting to get through passport control.

"All right, mate?" he asks the passport man when it's our turn.

The man nods, peers into the car and then starts checking our passports, one by one. Mikey's tapping gets louder and more and more impatient and Mum starts switching her diamond rings from one finger to another.

"Can we go home?" I whisper.

"Ssshhh, baby," says Mum, leaning over and stroking my head with a hard hand, "Nearly there."

The man hands the passports back to Mikey and waves us on.

"Phew," sighs Mikey, relaxing as we pull away.

"Yay!" shrieks Mum, frantically jiggling my hand up and down. "Freedom, Tiff! Freedom!"

Suddenly, some policemen step in front of the car and wave us over to one side. Mikey starts tap, tap, tapping on the steering wheel again and Mum starts fidgeting with her hair.

"Just a routine check, sir," says one of the policemen, leaning into the front window. "May we take another look at your passports, please?"

"Is this completely necessary?" says Mikey. "We need to board the ferry as soon as," he says, waving a hand toward me. "The kid needs the toilet; know what I mean?"

"I'm afraid it is necessary, sir, and we'll get you on board as soon as we can."

I feel really awake now, because something's not right. All the other cars are driving past us and climbing the ramp to board the ferry. But we're stuck here with policemen asking us questions. It's late and I want to be at home, asleep next to Chelsea, dreaming of *The Wizard of Oz* and Shirley Temple cocktails. I wish my mum had never had this stupid idea in the first place. I don't even *want* to go on holiday. I want my normal Saturday with Chels and me cosying up in bed, watching TV and eating ice cream straight from the tub. With Mum and me, together, wandering through the shops and buying cool stuff. Getting dressed up in new clothes and having lunch out, like ladies do. And we'd planned to take Chardonnay to the park. Everything is going wrong.

The policeman looks at me, scratches his head, and then turns to Mikey. "Are you the registered keeper of this vehicle, sir?"

"Yes mate," says Mikey, tapping and tapping. "It's

all in order, officer, I just bought it from my brother-in-law, he must have forgotten to send off the papers."

The policeman scratches his head again and I wonder if he has nits, like Chels and I had in the summer. "If you'd like to get out of the vehicle, sir, and step this way."

Mikey groans and opens the door. Mum lets out a wounded-dog squeal and starts rocking backwards and forwards humming the white cliffs of Dover song. Then we're surrounded by blue flashing lights, and I know that *Crimewatch* was true and that Chelsea was right. A large ball of worry drops into my tummy and wobbles around, and a sharp lump sticks in my throat. I start tap, tap, tapping and humming the white cliffs of Dover song too because now I really know that my mum's in trouble. Big trouble. And what about me?

All the doors are pulled open. There are policemen everywhere and handcuffs are snapped on to Mikey and Mum.

"Mum!" I call from the back seat, "Mum, what's happening?"

"It's all right, babe, Mama's here, no worries," her voice trembles as someone guides her towards a police car. "You and me, Tiff," she calls through the rain.

"You and me, Mum." I call back, panicking. "You and me."

I watch my mum pulling and struggling against the policemen. She starts screaming at them and fighting, and I wish they knew how to soothe her tantrums.

A lady police officer climbs into the car and sits next to me. "I'm Benita," she says. "What's your name, love?"

"Tiffany," I sniff. "What's happening to my mum?"

"I'm really sorry, Tiffany," she says, handing me a tissue, "we have to take your mum and dad into custody for a bit. There's some stuff that's happened and we just need to check it all out." She's trying to sound cheerful and reassuring. "We'll have you all back together as soon as we can."

"He's not my dad," I say, "he's my mum's business partner."

Then, before I know it, I'm in a police car, and my little wheelie suitcase is in the back. My mum's in another car being driven away from me, with blue lights flashing. I don't even know where Dover is and I need the toilet and Chardonnay is wriggling in the bag. The large ball keeps rolling around in my tummy, making me feel like I'm going to be sick. I can't stop my hand tap, tap, tapping on the car window and the white cliffs of Dover song is spinning through my mind, like it's got stuck in my brain.

"Where are you from, Tiffany?" Benita asks.

"London," I say.

"Is there anyone we can call for you, love? Your dad, maybe, or grandparents, aunts or uncles, friends?"

"There's my school friend, Chelsea," I sniff, "but her dad's really angry with my mum."

"Anyone else?"

I shake my head. "No one," I say. "Just me and Mum."

Chapter 6

A whole lake of tears is welling. . .

We drive to the police station. Benita shows me to the toilets and then sits me in a room with a brown plastic table and orange chairs. Chardonnay's still wriggling but she hasn't made a sound yet. She's such a good dog.

"Can I get you a cup of tea, or some water?"

"No thanks," I say. "When can I see my mum and go home?"

"Tiffany," she says, kneeling down beside me and taking my hand, "I'm really sorry, but we have to keep Mum here for a bit; until things are sorted out."

"What about me?" I croak.

"Well," she says, in a trying-to-be-kind voice, "as it's so late and there's no one for us to call at this stage, we've had to ask social services to send a social worker who will find somewhere for you to stay tonight. Then tomorrow we'll be able to take a fresh look at things. Mum knows what's happening to you and she knows that you'll be safe."

A whole lake of tears wells and quivers up through my body and tries to escape from my eyes. But I won't let it. I blink a lot and sniff into the tissue. Then I hear my mum's voice screaming away in another room, saying lots of swear words, calling out for me. Chardonnay hears her too because she starts scrabbling about in the bag. I pat her down to try and keep her quiet.

"What have you got in there, love?" asks Benita.

"Nothing."

"Sure?" she asks, not believing me. And then Chardonnay takes a leap and starts yelping and my bag tumbles to the ground.

Benita picks up the bag and takes a peep inside.

"Look what we've got in here," she says, holding Chardonnay in the air. Then Chardonnay decides that she can't hold on to her wee any more and it trickles on to the floor.

"Sorry," I say.

"No problem, Tiffany, I'll buzz for someone to come and mop it up."

Benita presses a red button on the wall.

"As for you," she says, ruffling Chardonnay's fluff, "I'm afraid we're going to have to put you in kennels for the night."

My lake of tears starts pushing up again. I blink hard because I won't let myself cry.

"Can't she come with me?" I ask, "Please? We only just got her and she hasn't even had one whole night with us yet."

"I'm sorry, but no one will take on you *and* a puppy as an emergency at this time of night. But don't you worry, we'll take good care of her – promise."

The lump in my throat rises up again and I can't swallow it down. Now I know how Dorothy from *The Wizard of Oz* feels when the nasty neighbour tries to take her dog, Toto, away. I can't lose my puppy, not now that I've finally got her. Why can't my mum sort this mess out and take us home? Surely there's something she can do? Chardonnay'll be scared. And lonely.

I can hear my mum's voice travelling down the corridor. She's screaming and shouting and having one of her full-blown temper tantrums.

"If I could just see my mum before I go, I'd be able to calm her down for you," I say quietly.

"I'm not sure it's allowed," Benita says.

"Please?"

A teeny river pushes its way out and stings my cheek. I rub my eye pretending I have an eyelash in it.

Benita pats my shoulder. "You stay here and I'll see what I can do, I'll just be a sec."

She leaves the room and my ears fill with the sound of keys clattering and doors clunking and Mum shouting. I look at my watch. It's one o'clock in the morning.

"You can have five minutes," says Benita, coming back into the room, "I've spoken to the sergeant and he says you can pop in to say a quick goodnight to your mum."

I feel all jelly again, and I'm shaking all over. My heart's pounding. We walk down the grey corridor towards my mum's shouting. Benita thumps the door,

I hear some keys jangling and we're in. I fly into Mum's arms and we squeeze each other tight, holding on, not wanting to let go.

"I'm sorry, baby," she sobs into my hair, "I'm so, so, sorry."

I cling on, breathe in her smell, and snuggle into her warmth.

"Don't leave me," I whisper. "Please don't leave me, Mum."

She sobs and sobs and I worry that she'll never be able to stop. She clings on so tight that her nails dig in. The big policeman standing near the door coughs and I remember that I don't have long to make her feel better.

"Remember your mascara, Mum," I say. I lick my tissue and mop up her face. "You don't want to go around looking like a mess, do you? What would Bianca say, eh, Mum?"

She pulls herself together. I untangle her hair, take her face in my hands and kiss her on the nose.

"Now come on, Mum, all this screaming and shouting isn't going to get us anywhere, is it?" I soothe.

"Sorry, Tiff," she sniffs, "I'll be good. I promise. It was all Mikey's fault. You do believe me, Tiff, don't you? Just give me a bit of time to sort this mess out and we'll be back home together before you can say 'wizard'."

I don't know what to believe any more. But I know it's not normal to be in a police station with my mum in the middle of the night. And I know I'm the only one in the world who can calm her down. And I'm boiling mad inside because our life is *always* about her.

"What about me?" I whisper. "What happens to me and Chardonnay while you're sorting it all out?"

"I promise you, Tiff, it won't be for long and I'll come and pick you both up as soon as I can."

"But, Mum, please!"

"There's nothing I can do, babe. Nothing."

Suddenly a brilliant idea pops into my mind. "Except. . . except maybe you could telephone someone. . . on Sark?"

"Don't even go there, Tiff, I've told you before."

"But it has to be worth a try, Mum, please?"

"Oh, I don't know, Tiff, it's been too long. They may have moved away years ago. I can't just call out of the blue when I'm in trouble and ask for help, can I?"

"But, Mum, this is about me as well. It's not just about you. I'm going to be sent off to a foster home, alone. They're *my* family too, they're not just yours."

My mum drags her hand through her hair.

"OK," she sniffs, "I'll do my best, Tiff, I promise."

The policeman tells us our time is up. I put the plug in my feelings and pull away. "Now be good and do what they tell you," I say. "No more tantrums."

"No more tantrums," Mum echoes.

Benita takes hold of my hand and heads for the door; Mum holds the other one, not wanting to let me go. They're both hanging on, tugging gently. Mum's hand and mine slide apart until we're just touching fingertips, until there's just space between us, and then she crumples in a heap on her orange chair.

"I love you, babe," she whispers.

"I love you, Mum."

Chapter 7

So I need you to trust me...

A man in a funny hat comes into the room where me and Benita are still waiting. Chardonnay is on my lap. Her little body keeps trembling and she's looking all lost and worried. In one day she's gone from being cosy at home with her mum and puppy brothers and sisters to being in a police room, on her way to the kennels. I hold her close wishing she were small enough to climb inside my pocket and come with me, wherever I'm going. Benita yawns, sips her hot tea and shakes hands with the man.

"Hi, Tiffany," he says. He holds out his hand for me to shake. "Sorry I took so long to get to you." He pulls up an orange chair and sits really close to me. "I know this must all be very difficult for you, Tiffany, and there's a lot for you to take in," he says. "My name's Amida and I'm your social worker. It's my job to make sure that you're safe tonight, until we've sorted somewhere else for you. I'm going to take you to a lovely family, where you can get some sleep and something to eat. Your mum knows that we're taking good care of you, so I need you to trust me. Do you have any questions, Tiffany?"

I shake my head. I have at least seven million questions whizzing through my brain about what's happening in my life and why my mum's in a police station crying. And about what has *actually* happened and what Mikey did. And if someone from Sark will come and find me and if they do what will they be like. But all my questions are squashed together in the little worry bag that's stuck in my throat.

"Great then," he says, standing up, yawning. "Let's get you to bed."

Benita hands him my wheelie suitcase and takes Chardonnay from my lap. Chardonnay wriggles and yelps, trying to get back to me. She looks really worried about what's happening, so I stroke her head to calm her down. I want to give her a kiss goodbye, but I can't trust that my feelings won't spill out all over the place. I give her one last pat, take a very deep breath to keep everything under control and stand up on my jelly legs.

"I promise she'll be well looked after," calls Benita as we leave the room.

Amida's car smells of leather and peppermints. He offers me one but I shake my head, I don't want it. He tucks a cosy blanket around me to warm me up and calm my chattering teeth, and does up my seatbelt to save me the trouble.

"The people you're going to be staying with are called Darren and Claudia – you'll like them; they'll be up waiting for us. I've already told them all about you." He yawns. "It's been a long old night for you, eh?"

I don't have any voice left tonight, not for anyone. And even if I did, why would I want to talk to some nosy old social worker about how I'm feeling and how long my night has been? It's not like he's really interested, is it? He's just doing his job and trying to be kind. But I don't need kind, I need my life back. What does he even expect me to say? Some sad old story about how my whole entire life has been ruined in one night, just so he can feel sorry for me? Or about how I'm starting to feel really angry with my mum? Well, whatever it is he wants from me he's not getting it. No one is. My mouth is staying firmly zipped.

"Here we are," says Amida, parking the car in front of a big house, "I'll come back to see you in the morning, Tiffany. I hope you sleep well."

A man wearing tracksuit bottoms and an old woolly jumper comes out of the house, followed by a lady in a pink-and-white spotted dressing gown. Amida pulls my wheelie suitcase from the boot of his car.

"Thanks for this," he says to them. "Sorry it's such short notice."

The car door is opened for me and the lady, Claudia, helps me out. My legs feel heavy and I want to lie down.

"Welcome, Tiffany," she gushes, taking hold of me and guiding me along the dark path. "Let's get you tucked up in bed shall we?"

I hear Amida drive away and am left alone with two more new people to get used to. I follow them into the house and have some milk and biscuits without a fuss.

Claudia takes me into a green bedroom that has a blue rug on the floor and a yellow teddy on the bed. She helps me into my pyjamas and carries on chatting away, not minding that I'm not joining in. I clean my teeth with weird-tasting toothpaste.

"Night then, Tiffany," says Darren, popping his head round the door. "We're just in the room next to you, so if you need anything in the night, or if you're worried and need to talk, just come and wake us up, OK?"

Claudia's soft hands tuck me in. She leaves my door open a bit so a sliver of landing light can peep its way in. Shadows hang on my walls and strange sounds creak and creep around me. New fabric-softener smells sit in my nose and tickle my face. And when it's safe and quiet and there's no one around, the tears sneak out of my eyes. They trickle at first and then a dark monster in my stomach lurches up and pushes hard. My face crumples like a stupid piece of rubbish paper and my voice wants to call out for my mum and Chardonnay. But I won't let it call, and I won't let it call for stupid Darren or stupid Claudia either. Instead, I bite hard on the yellow teddy and try to sleep.

Chapter 8

Today is not happening...

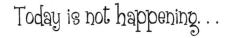

I keep waking up in the night and have to keep reminding myself where I am. When I open my eyes in the morning Claudia is standing there.

"Good morning, Tiffany," she says, sitting on the edge of my bed. "Did you sleep well?" I shrug, ignore her questions, and try to find the safe place in my head where my life hasn't been ruined. She doesn't seem to mind that I'm not answering her and just carries on jabbering away. "Amida is popping back this morning, Tiffany, to have a chat and let you know what's happening. Why don't you have a shower and some breakfast and get yourself ready for the day?"

She takes me out into the hallway and introduces me to the girl in the next room. "This is Matilda," says Claudia, "she's the same age as you. She'll show you the ropes, OK?"

"I only need to know where the shower is," I say to Matilda when Claudia has gone. "I don't need to see anything else. I'm being picked up soon."

Matilda steps forward and grabs my arm, hard. "Wake up, new girl," she sneers. "We're all here for ever. No one's coming back for you, no one wants you around any more; this is the rubbish dump and you've been dumped here, just like the rest of us. So get used to it."

"You're wrong," I say, trying to stare her out, "someone is coming for me, soon." But she's good at staring, very good. She's better than Chelsea, better than me. My stupid tummy turns to jelly again. Matilda pushes me into the bathroom, slams the door behind us and shows me her fist.

"See this?" she says. "You just make sure you don't get in my way, otherwise my fist might find itself bumping into your teeth."

"You won't need to worry about me for long," I

brave, staring at her with hard eyes, to hide my fear. "I told you, I'm getting out of here soon. Very soon."

But she just makes a rude sign at me and walks out.

I run the shower – hot. Is Matilda right? Am I on the rubbish dump for good? I wet a pink flannel in the hot water and bite the fluff hard while my body trembles and more tears sneak from my eyes. I panic that I might never be able to stop because my tears just keep coming and coming. I'm worried that Matilda is outside the door, listening with her big ugly ears. So I make the shower go freezing cold to wake me up and try to think about more happy stuff, like the old film, *Singing in the Rain*. I pretend I'm holding a big black umbrella and I tipadee-tap-dance around the shower and try to make myself smile.

While I'm getting dressed I decide that today is actually not happening. I start rubbing all the horribleness out and try filling my mind with pictures of wonderful days and beautiful things. Like my mum on a good day when she's all happy and we're having a lovely time together at the funfair or the ice-skating rink. Like how happy she looks when she's bought herself a new ring or when she's spinning around on a pair of shiny, new high-heeled shoes in a cloud of special perfume. And I try to remember her soft face when we're snuggling in bed together, sharing secrets. But scary pictures of my mum in a police cell, and Chardonnay in kennels, and Mikey with his fat cigars, and blue flashing lights, and peppermints, and a small island with an unknown family keep crowding in.

Amida the social worker is a liar. He's not coming to see me today like he promised. Instead he spoke to Darren on the phone and said that nothing much could be done with me until after the weekend, so I have to stay here until then. I've turned into a hot-potato problem that no one wants to touch. Matilda *is* right and I hate her for that. She makes a big fat 'told you so' face at me later on when we're climbing into Darren's car to go to the cinema. Then she 'accidentally' sticks her stupid clumsy foot out so that I trip and smash my shin on the cold metal. Nobody has noticed that I might not be in a cinema kind of mood. Or that it's super-weird for me to be living in this stupid place. No one has mentioned the fact that my mum is locked behind a grey door, crying, or that I might be feeling left alone. The truth is a bad fart smell in the room that everyone is too polite to mention. None of the other kids is saying why they got left here on the rubbish dump either.

Claudia waves us off, smiling, with a baby under her arm, like we're her own children going out with our own dad. But I've never even been to the cinema with my own dad before, because I've never even seen him with my own eyes and I don't even know his name, so it's a stupid thing to pretend. I decide that Claudia is a liar too, just like everyone else in my new life. And I bet that when we've gone she just heaves a big sigh of relief because she's getting rid of us all for a few hours.

Everyone is pretending to be having a nice time with Darren and the helper person that's come along with us, when they'd really rather be somewhere else.

I want to watch the new '12' film but I don't trust Matilda's fists in the dark.

"I want to see the Disney film with the little ones," I lie.

"Are you sure?" asks Darren.

I nod and Matilda sticks her thumb in her mouth

and makes a stupid baby face at me. I pretend not to notice and get busy showing the little ones the big cardboard Disney pictures in the foyer. Darren gets us some popcorn and some juice. He's says Coke's not allowed because it's bad for us, but that's what me and Mum always have, so I don't see the problem, really. When the Disney colours flash across the screen I try to find a gentle place in my mind; a place that's somewhere "Over the Rainbow", with no blue flashing lights or *Crimewatch* or lost Mums or spiteful Matildas. A place where there's no waiting or wondering what might happen to you and no pretending that you're OK, when you really have an earthquake going on inside you all of the time.

My mind starts drifting off and I'm thinking about my friend Chelsea. I really want to text her and tell her what's happening to me, but I feel too embarrassed for anyone to know, even her. It's obvious that I'm not going to be in school on Monday and I'm worried that if I tell her she might just let my news slip out of her mouth at lunch break. Then the gossip would spread around that my mum was in a police cell, being accused of doing bad things. And even worse, everyone would know that I'd been left here on the rubbish dump, alone, waiting to be rescued. So I have no choice. I have to wait and see what's going to happen. But if I don't text Chelsea as usual then she'll wonder where I am and her imagination will go crazy. Especially as she saw Mikey's face all over *Crimewatch*. There's nothing else for it. I'll have to think of a lie.

Chapter 9

A lie to my Bestie. . .

That night, I creep up the stairs and slide away to my room.

I have to put my plan into action before Chelsea gets too suspicious, so I pull my mobile from my bag and ping it into life. I look through my photos and delete the one of Mikey's big fat face, then I look at a photo of my mum. Every time I think about her, the washing machine starts up in my tummy. Something deep inside me knows that she and Mikey have done something bad, but still a small part of me wants to believe that the police have made a huge mistake. Somehow, I always knew that something like this would happen. But I never imagined how it would feel. I try to convince myself that I do not miss my mum. In fact, right now, I think I actually hate her and never want to see her again. I curl up in a tiny ball, trying to hide from the world. I open a photo of Chardonnay. Looking at her puppy face makes tiny tears escape from my eyes again, but they mustn't, so I kiss her quick, zip away my feelings and get started on my text.

Hi, r u there? xxxxxxxxxxxxxxxxxxxx

I press send and wait.

Yeh, where r u? xxxxxxxxxxxxxxxxxxxxxx

A lie to my bestie.

I'm in France on holiday, in a cool hotel. Been drinking Shirley Temples by the pool all day. What r u doing? Missing u more than all the stars in the sky. xxxxxxxxxxxxxxxxxx

I press send. I have never lied to Chels before. We're besties, forever. We've always told each other the truth, all our worries and all our secrets. But I can't tell her this. Not ever. It'll all be sorted out soon enough and Mum and I will be home and Chels will never have to know.

In France? My dad says they caught Mikey and your mum. It's in the news. He's v angry and says I can't talk to u any more. Missing u 2 more than all the cherry drops in the cherry drop shop. xxxxxxxxxxxxxxxx

My mouth goes dry and I can't swallow. My heart starts thumping in my ears.

They did get him. He's rubbish, but my mum and I r in France. R we still besties? Missing u more and more and more than all the stars in the skies and more than all the lemon meringue pies. xxxxxxxxxxxxxxxxxxxxxxxx

I hit the send button and wait.

Have fun. Hope you don't have to eat frogs' legs! Besties for life xxxxxxxxxxxxxxxxxxxx

Yuck! Don't worry, I won't! Tell school I'll be back soon. Besties for life 2, forever and ever xxxxxxxxxxxxxxxxxxxx

My door creaks open and a long shadow stretches its way across the carpet. I know it's not Claudia or Darren coming to say goodnight, or a little one looking for cuddles.

"They'll all leave you," Matilda says, "I promise you. The texts will stop. They'll all forget about you. Everyone else's life will go on happily, except for yours. No one wants to be friends with a rubbish-dump girl. It happens to us all, so get used to it – fast. This is the dead zone, new girl. The end of love."

I close my phone and throw it in my bag because she's right, and I know that Matilda is the only one in the house who's telling the truth.

"And you'll never forget," she taunts. "You wait, it happens to us all. You'll play it over and over in your mind, trying to work it out. You'll have your very own horror movie etched on your memory bank forever."

Please, please don't let her be right.

Chapter 10

I've got some news for you...

"I've got some news for you, Tiffany," says Amida when he arrives on Monday morning. He pops a peppermint into his mouth. "Come and sit down."

I sit at the kitchen table and sip my juice. He does that stupid thing again where he sits really close to me and looks deep into my eyes. "I'm afraid that your mum's going to have to stay in police custody for a bit longer than we thought. There's good news though, Tiffany. She's arranged for you to stay with your family on Sark." My tummy starts churning. He breathes peppermint breath in my face. "Your mum's managed to get hold of her sister, your Auntie Cass, and she's coming to pick you up this afternoon."

My head starts spinning. I know I suggested that my mum telephoned Sark, but I didn't think about what might happen if someone came to get me. I didn't think that I'd *actually* be going to stay with them. What I really thought was that she'd be home by now and that I'd be back at school on Monday morning and no one would ever have to know anything about the worst weekend of my life. What are my family on Sark like? My mum always said it was the most boring place on the planet! And I don't know even where I'll be living or what school I'll be going to or what's going to happen to me. But *someone is coming to get me soon.*

I leave Amida drinking coffee with Claudia and fly upstairs to the green room. I stuff my clothes into my wheelie suitcase. Matilda was wrong. I'm not a rubbish-dump kid after all; somebody in this stupid world cares about me, even if my own mother doesn't! I put my case near the front door and sit on the tatty old sofa in the hallway.

"She won't be here for hours, Tiffany," says Claudia. "Why don't you find something to do to pass the time?"

But I'm not moving. No way. As far as I can see,

rubbish-dump kids don't get rescued very often and I'm not about to miss my opportunity for escape. And I have a lot of thinking to do. What will my Auntie Cass be like? How long will I have to stay with her? Will I even like her? And what about Chardonnay? My brain is a fairground ride, spinning and spinning. I pick and pick at the little frayed strands of sofa fabric and make tiny plaits to pass the time. I wait and wait. At lunchtime Claudia brings me a cheese and tomato toastie and some juice. The baby is having a nap so she does that sitting-really-close-to-me, looking-into-my-eyes thing, like Amida.

"How are you feeling, Tiffany?" she asks, sipping on her coffee.

It's a stupid question. In the past three days my whole life has turned into a crumbling tower and I know that she's trying to squirrel away into my feelings again. But I don't want it, so I put them in a safe box, tuck them inside my heart and hide away the key. "I'm fine," I say. "Really fine."

I'm still waiting when Darren brings the kids home from school. Matilda slumps down on the sofa next to me. "So it's true, you really are going then?"

"I am," I say. "My auntie's coming to pick me up." I want to say "I told you so, you horrible girl" and I want to hurt her and scare her and get my own back, but her face looks so sad that I can't bring myself to do it. She waits and waits with me, and the more I think about it, the more I begin to see that Matilda isn't a horrible girl at all; she's a hurt girl, a left-alone girl. I start to understand how hurt feelings can sometimes come out all twisted and wrong and make people do horrible things like lying to their best friend.

"I wish I could come," she sighs. "I wish I could drink some magic shrinking potion and climb in your bag. No one would notice."

We sit in silence, busy with our thoughts. After ages and ages someone knocks at the door. I freeze and wait for Darren to open it. My heart's thumping away. I smooth my hair down and paint on a smile. And suddenly, Amida appears in the doorway with a woman who looks like a brown-haired version of my mum. The lump grows in my throat again, making it hard to swallow. My eyes don't know where to look and I don't know what to do. I needn't have worried, because my Auntie Cass takes charge.

"Wow," she says, looking at Matilda, and me. "I don't need to be told which one of you is Tiffany, do I? Look at you," she says pulling me to my feet and folding me into her arms. "You look exactly like your mum did when she was your age. I can't believe it!" She cups my face in her hands and takes a good look at me, tears rolling down her cheeks. "I'm so excited to meet you, Tiff, so glad you're safe. I didn't even know you'd been born until your mum phoned me." My throat lump starts aching and tears are pricking at my eyes. I push them down, and push her away. I can't let myself cry, not know.

"Can we go?" I whisper.

"You, bet," she says.

Claudia, Darren and Amida say goodbye to me and wish me luck. Matilda's face turns into thunder and rain. "You're so lucky," she says, rubbing her eyes.

"I know," I say, giving her cold hand a warm squeeze, "and I think you will be too, one day."

And I just hope that I am right.

Chapter 11

My Aunt Cass drops the bombshell. . .

"We've got so much to sort out, Tiff, and not a lot of time," says Auntie Cass when we're settled in her car. "But first let's go and find somewhere to eat and I'll fill you in on what's happening."

We drive to the centre of town and find an Italian place where we order pepperoni pizza, cheesy garlic bread and a big salad. While we're waiting for our food to arrive my Auntie Cass drops the bombshell.

"I'm so sorry to have to tell you, Tiff," she says, holding my hands in hers, "but it looks like your mum is going to have to go to prison for a few months. She's really sorry and she says to tell you that if she could change things she would. She loves you millions and is always thinking about you. She's asked me if I would take care of you while she's away and I've said yes. So you're coming home with me, back to Sark, where you belong right now."

My heart turns to ice. "She can't love me that much," I snap, "otherwise she wouldn't have got us into this mess in the first place, would she? And she never thinks about me, not really, she only ever thinks about herself and what she wants. What did she actually do, anyway?" I ask. "Can you tell me what *actually* happened?"

"Well," she says, looking worried, "I don't want to worry you, but I think you deserve to know the truth about what's going on. It looks like your mum got herself involved with a bad crowd. They've been accused of stealing some pretty big things, by all accounts, and for using other people's credit cards. And trying to get on a ferry to leave the country just made things worse."

"I knew it. She always does it," I bark. "Everywhere we go, it's like she just can't help herself. I thought she was getting up to some dodgy stuff; it was Mikey wasn't it and that stupid red car? She's so embarrassing.

I hate her. And what about Chardonnay? What's going to happen to her?"

Auntie Cass's face drops. "Tiff," she says, trying to comfort me by holding my hand, "I'm afraid that the money your mum used to buy her was money she made from the stolen car. The police need to reclaim the cash, so Chardonnay's had to go back to the breeder you bought her from. I'm so sorry."

"It's not fair," I whisper. "None of this is fair." I pull my hand away and stuff it in my pocket, her words still stinging. The little box where I'd hidden my feelings unlocks itself. Hot tears spill down my cheeks and my whole body trembles. Our waiter brings us our food, but Auntie Cass pushes it to one side and pulls me into a hug. I pull back, trying to sniff it all away, trying to be brave. But my tears keep coming and coming in great fat sobs and as hard as I try, I just can't hold them in any more. I want to just scream it all out, and break all the plates and trash all the food. I want to punch and bite and scratch and kick someone. I want to push it all away and scrunch it all up and throw myself in the bin. My explosion of rage travels up through my body, wanting to escape me, wanting to be free. My feet scuffle and stomp on the floor and my fists curl like Matilda's, ready to fight. But my auntie just pulls me back into her hug and holds me close.

"It's OK, Tiff," she whispers into my hair. "It's OK."

"But it's not," I scream, pulling myself away from her hug. "My life is never going to be OK again."

After our food we drive away from Dover, back to London, back to our flat to collect my things before going off to Sark. Auntie Cass picked up the keys from my mum when she'd visited her in the police station. Apparently, my mum is going to be moved to a proper prison soon, where she'll have to wait until some judge person decides how long she'll have to stay there for. If she hadn't tried to run away she'd be allowed home to wait for the judge's decision, but now they have to lock her up in case she tries to run again. I decide it's about time I stopped being pushed around by everyone and make some decisions of my own. And my first decision is that I'm not going to visit her in prison. Or even speak to her on the phone.

It feels weird going home without my mum. And it's scary when we open the door. The dresses that Chels and I borrowed are still strewn across the room and the

Shirley Temple mess is still sticky on the table. But there's other mess too. Someone has been rummaging through our drawers and has tipped our stuff out all over the floor. And there are big empty spaces where our sofa and TV and stereo used to be. I freeze.

"It's OK, Tiff," Auntie Cass soothes. "Your mum warned me that things might look bad. The police let themselves in, they were searching for stolen goods and it looks like they found what they were looking for. Sorry I didn't warn you before."

I run to my room and loads of my stuff has gone. My laptop, my stereo and TV, my iPods and my jewellery, even my bed. I'm glad everything's gone. I don't even want her stolen stuff, her shiny stuff, her new, new, new stuff. Doesn't she know that I don't care about having new things all the time? Doesn't she know that having a mum who looks after me is way more important than junk that will soon be thrown on the rubbish dump? Just like me.

Auntie Cass starts sorting me a pile of clothes and folding them into a black bin liner.

"I don't want them," I say, "I don't want any of this."

Auntie Cass leaves the clothes and heads for the door.

Anger-bubbles fizz through my body, and my bottom lip trembles.

"Why did she do it?" I whisper.

"I don't know, Tiff."

I gather up my special set of old movies and my ruby slippers that Chelsea bought me last Christmas and shove them in my bag. There's one more thing I want and it's in my bedside drawer. Everything else can stay.

Chapter 12

It's time to go...

"There's something I have to do," I say, while we're locking up.

I lead the way to Chelsea's flat, take a deep breath and knock on the door. Lying about things isn't going to help and lying to friends is especially bad. As far as I can see, lies just get people into trouble. It's time to face the truth.

"What do you want?" says her dad's boiling-mad face. "I told Chels that I didn't want her speaking to you any more."

"Dad," says Chelsea barging her way through, "stop it, leave her alone." And then we're hugging each other

tight, Chelsea and me, besties forever.

"I came to say goodbye," I say. "I'm sorry Chels, I lied to you, we weren't in France, you were right, my mum's in big trouble and I have to go away. But I wanted to give you this." I give her the special heart-necklace from my bedside table, the one I bought on our school trip in Year Six. "You know," I say. "To remember me by."

"And you have this," she says, pulling off her favourite silver ring and putting it on my finger. "I'll never forget you, Tiff," she smiles. "Never ever. Hey, let's make a pact, let's meet up at Tiffany's when we're seventeen – at twelve o'clock on Valentine's Day. Promise?"

"Promise," I say. "Besties forever?" Her Dad's patience runs out and he goes to slam the door in my face.

"Besties forever, Tiff," Chelsea shouts back.

"Come on," says my Auntie Cass. "It's time to go."

After a really long drive we stop in some place called Weymouth. Auntie Cass finds a hotel and books us in for the night. I've fallen asleep in the car and haven't realised that it's way past midnight. It feels like my brain's shutting down. My thoughts and worries sit heavy on my cloudy head.

In the morning we have some breakfast then make our way to the dock where we'll catch the ferry to an island called Guernsey. From there you get another ferry to Sark. The November chill slaps itself around our cheeks and icy-grey water laps the sides of the ferry. Once we've bought our tickets we get back in the car, turn the heating on full and wait in the queue to get on the boat. My tummy starts its washing machine thing again, going round and round, spinning tighter and tighter. My hand starts tap, tap, tapping on the window while I'm watching the rain. I'm nervous. The last time I was in a ferry queue, things didn't exactly turn out so well.

The ferry is full of white-haired old people going on holiday and businessmen in smart suits. It isn't half term, or anything, so there are no other kids around. My Auntie Cass doesn't keep staring into my eyes like the others did and she doesn't squirrel away at my feelings. She lets me get used to the fact that my old life is moving further and further away from me with every choppy wave we sail over. Occasionally she gives my hand a friendly squeeze, or strokes my hair or sends me a reassuring smile. But I ignore her. I'm never trusting anyone in my whole life, ever again. We buy some drinks and one of those puzzle books and she tries to get me interested in working out the clues. But I'm not interested in her stupid puzzle book. Mum and I laugh at people who are interested in stuff like that. We like glossy magazines full of cool, fun stuff and celebrity gossip. I sigh. What will life be like on an island where people like puzzle books?

Chapter 13

Some welly boots. . .

"Right," says Auntie Cass, once we arrive in Guernsey. "We've a couple of hours before we catch the Sark ferry and quite a lot to do." We park the car and head off towards the shops. "Life on Sark is a bit different," she continues, "so you'll need some new clothes." She doesn't mention the fact that I'd refused to take any of my clothes from home.

At least Guernsey has good shops. Auntie Cass buys me a few new outfits, some underwear and a new pair of pyjamas. Then we go into a shop that's full of sailing and boaty things.

"It rains a lot on Sark," she says, "so you need proper wet-weather gear, you know, a jacket and boots."

"I'm not wearing one of those," I gruff, when Auntie Cass pulls an anorak thing off the shelf.

"Well, you'll have to get something," she says, "or you're going to get very wet."

Eventually I choose a red sailing jacket with a big hood that's OKish because it has these bright flowers all over the lining. But Wellington boot buying is different. I haven't worn wellies since I was about six years old, which I think is a good age to stop wearing them. But Auntie Cass has a very different opinion.

"Everyone wears them on Sark," she says, noticing my worried face. "We have to, there aren't any proper roads, and when it rains, it really rains and everything gets covered in mud. Don't worry, you'll fit in, Tiff, I promise."

I'm not worried about fitting in. I'd rather fit out. Who wants to 'fit in' to a place where they all wear wellies and it rains all the time? My mum was right to leave Sark. I can't ever imagine *her* wearing stupid boots and anoraks. She wouldn't be seen dead in them. But I don't have any choice about anything in my life any more. So I find myself trying on wellies and flopping about with massive welly feet. I'm not interested in them but Auntie Cass insists that I choose. I go for red ones covered with little cream polka dot hearts. They're OK, I suppose.

My mum told me once that cars weren't allowed on Sark, but I didn't know that there aren't actually any proper roads. I start worrying about what all the other kids will be like. Will they all be boring old country bumpkin turnips who know nothing about anything? Will they have heard of things like computers or the internet? Do they even know that mobile phones have been invented?

"Do you have electricity on Sark," I ask, "or do you still have to use candles?"

Auntie Cass cracks up laughing. "It's OK, Tiff," she laughs, "we haven't been left in the Dark Ages, we're part of the modern world, you know. Yes, we do have electricity. And telephones and inside toilets. And speaking of telephones, have you got a mobile?"

I nod.

"All the kids on Sark have them because you'll be out and about all the time. It's a really safe place to live – not like London, and all the kids have loads of freedom."

My washing machine spin turns into an excited flutter and I can't help it. Apart from leaving me in our flat alone, my mum has always been really over-protective of me. She says it's not safe for me to go out on my own in London because you never know what might happen. But what does she care about me now? I can go wandering off with anyone I like, and she won't even know.

"I know you're feeling upset, Tiff, and it's to be expected. Your whole life has just been turned upside down. But I promise you're going to love it on Sark. I just know it. Everyone there knows your mum, and if she'd stayed on the island then you'd have grown up there too. You'll take to it like a duck to water, you'll see, especially when we get you on a bike and signed up at the school."

"I don't even know how to ride a bike," I scowl.

"You've never ridden a bike?" she smiles. "What about a pony?"

I shake my head. I obviously have a lot to learn.

"Well, everyone has a bike on Sark. It's the best way to get around."

"I'll walk," I say. "That's why I've got legs."

Auntie Cass ignores my remark and we go into a café for hot chocolate and some food. Then we dash into a kids' shop where she buys a pair of pink fairy-wings and a sparkly wand.

"For your cousin, Indigo," she smiles. "She's only five and she's dying to meet you."

"I didn't know I had a cousin."

"I didn't know I had a niece. Suddenly both our families are a little bit bigger."

We return the car to the car-hire place and hurry to catch the ferry to Sark. There are loads of people waiting at the dock and as we join them everyone's eyes land on me. I stare at the ground, my face turning into a hot tomato.

"This is Tiff," Auntie Cass announces, "Carla's daughter, my niece. She's coming to stay."

"You didn't really need to introduce her, Cass," says a lady with a warm smile, "she's the image of her mother. I would have recognised her a mile off. It's incredible."

Almost everyone agrees, and as we all pile on to the little Sark ferry they start clucking around me like old hens, asking me all sorts of questions about my mum and myself. Luckily, Auntie Cass answers all the difficult questions about how my mum is and why she hasn't been home to visit for so long, which luckily means that I don't have to.

"Carla's got some stuff to sort out in London," she says, "but she'll be joining us soon enough and we won't let her escape a second time, will we, Tiff?"

I stare straight ahead and ignore them all. My nose is full of diesel fumes, which make my tummy churn. And anyway I'm not interested in answering their nosy questions. There's one lady who doesn't ask anything. She's wearing a brown anorak and a sour-lemon face. She's crammed herself into the back seat of the ferry with a girl about my age, whose green eyes keep peeping at me from underneath her fringe.

"Let's go out on deck," says Auntie Cass, leading the way, "so you can see your new home."

The lady in the brown anorak mutters under her breath as we make for the deck. "The bad penny rolls home, then, eh? Well, well, well, I wonder what bother Carla Morris has got herself into this time?"

The green-eyed girl pokes her tongue slowly out of her mouth and points it at me. I send poison dagger eyes back.

"You keep your bitterness to yourself, Mandy, do you hear?" snaps Auntie Cass. "Leave her alone. And you, Holly."

"What was she saying?" I ask as we step out into the strong wind.

"Nothing, Tiff, really, don't you listen to her, she's just a bitter woman, that's all."

The cold wind nips our ears and licks our cheeks. I hold my arms wide open like Jack and Rose do in the film *Titanic* and I feel the wind rush through my fingers and through my hair. Auntie Cass pulls a camera out of her bag and takes a picture.

"This brings back so many memories," she sighs. "It feels like only yesterday that your mum and I were making this journey for the very first time. I was exactly your age, and your mum was eight." She wipes away a tear and a splash of sea-rain, "I've missed her so much, Tiff. I know things aren't easy for you, but I'm so glad you're here."

She edges closer and closer to me, wanting to be near. But I fold my arms and turn my face to the freezing, windy spray. I see the group of little islands getting nearer and nearer with each wave. They're like great rocks rising out of the sea, and for a second I see my new life as a completely empty white page, stretching out before me, waiting for me to fill it in.

Chapter 14

We have to walk from here. . .

"Take your first step on Sark soil," says Auntie Cass, guiding me off the ferry.

It doesn't look much like home to me. The dock is full of noisy tractors with rumbling engines and people are scurrying all over the place, taking cargo from the ferry and loading it on to tractors. Auntie Cass leads me to a tractor that has a trailer attached to it and we climb on board. I'm not exactly pleased to see that Mandy and her daughter, Holly, have joined us.

"I'll be keeping a good eye on you, Tiffany Morris," spits Mandy as we rumble our way up the steep black cliffs. "If you're anything like your mother you'll be too busy getting what you want for yourself to worry about other people's feelings. You leave my Holly alone, do you hear?"

"Mandy, I thought I told you to leave her out of it," says Auntie Cass. "The past has nothing to do with Tiffany. Give her a chance, she's a child."

"Give her a chance! You must be joking! After what Carla put me through? She ruined my life unless you forgot. And this one, she's her mother's daughter and you know it. Two peas in a pod. Trouble."

Holly pokes out her tongue at me again and gives me a nasty look. I'm glad that the tractor has stopped and we're getting out.

"We have to walk from here," says Auntie Cass, not mentioning Mandy's comments.

A dirt track takes us through a small row of old shops, which Auntie Cass says is the main street, called The Avenue. It doesn't look much like a main street to me. She keeps on chattering away, pointing everything out to me, and introducing me to people who cycle past. I can't take it all in. Everything seems blurry and unreal and her voice keeps getting lost in the wind. All I can hear is Mandy's harsh voice echoing round my mind. *The bad penny rolls home. . . She ruined my life. . .*

"What did she do?" I ask. "What did Mum do to Mandy?"

"Don't worry about it, Tiff, it was years ago. Don't let it spoil your first day here."

"How can you say that?" I shriek. "My day was spoiled before her. I want to know what happened. No wonder my mum never wanted to come back to this dump. I should never have asked her to call you."

Auntie Cass winces. I've hurt her and I don't care. Maybe Mandy's right, maybe I am trouble. In my mind I draw a big black smudge on the fresh white page of my new life. My mum isn't even here; she's miles away. A long drive and two ferry rides away. She hasn't even been here for thirteen years and yet she's still managing to ruin my day, ruin my new start, ruin my whole life. A thunderstorm of hatred brews away inside.

Everything around me looks muddy and bleak. Most of the shops are closed. Some of them have tourist stuff like teddies and ornaments with "Sark" written on them, all stuffed together. Some shops are closed for the whole winter and they look all dark and dingy and sad, waiting for spring. When the shops end there are just houses, a grey church and empty space.

Windswept fields, like in Dorothy's windy world, have bare trees in them that have grown bent and crooked from so much bad weather. It's quiet too, except for our footsteps crunching on the dirt, the occasional rumble of a tractor and the swish of the breeze. It's too quiet and that spooks me. This is a dead-land and I wonder what ghostly old people live behind the dark windows of the funny little houses. I long for London traffic jams and bright lights and red buses and loads of noise and open shops full of new things and shiny things and pizza places and beauty salons. I want piles of people bumping into me, busy people going somewhere, hopping into cars, running for trains. I long for my own home, how it used to be, and my own life and Chelsea and our *Wizard of Oz* nights. I long for anywhere but here.

"It's a bit different from London, I know," says Auntie Cass, reading my thoughts and ignoring the question about my mum. "I remember when we arrived we thought we'd been brought to the worst place in the world, to a desert land with nothing beyond. We kept planning to run back to London until our dad bought us ponies and we made new friends. Then we loved it here. You wait and see, you'll get used to it soon enough. Sark is like a beautiful jewel still hidden in the rock, waiting to be discovered."

She takes hold of my hand and gives it a friendly squeeze. I pull it away, stuff it back into my pocket and kick some random stones into the hedge.

"Look," she says, pointing to a long low building with a steep roof. "That's the Island Hall. The bit at the end is your new school and the rest is a café and community space where all sorts of fun things happen."

The thought of starting school and meeting more new people and having to face Holly's spiteful tongue every day turns my tummy into a hard ball. My brain feels squished and tight, like everything inside it is being pressed down, crowding in. It's busy trying to make sense of everything, trying to understand. I'm so tired, I want to run away and hide in a dark hole, with no one around. I want to run away to a land where Mums don't do bad things, somewhere over the rainbow where dreams come true. Matilda's gloomy words of warning dance round my brain. She was right. I will always remember this.

Always remember what my mum has done to our lives.

A quiet space grows between my Auntie Cass and me.
All our words have disappeared. Our footsteps crunch,
crunch, crunch, my suitcase drags and our shopping bags
crinkle and swish when they bang against our knees.
We make our way down a really long track, lined with
gnarly old trees. Finally, it opens out on to a cobbled
courtyard. Two grey stone buildings stand blinking in
the breeze.

"Here we are, Tiff," says Auntie Cass. "Welcome
home."

Chapter 15

A small silver picture frame keeps glinting. . .

"Muuummmyyy," shrieks a little girl, wrapping herself around Auntie Cass's legs. "You're home!"

Auntie Cass lifts her high into the air and swings her round and around, and thrusts the pink fairy-wings and wand into her hands.

"This is Indigo," says Auntie Cass, catching her breath and introducing us, "and Indigo, this is Tiff, your cousin."

I smile at the little fairy girl, because none of this is her fault. Indigo sticks her thumb into her mouth and buries a shy face into Auntie Cass's jumper.

"Say hello to Tiff," says Auntie Cass, "she's come to stay."

Indigo's big blue eyes peep through her dark curly fringe. "Gello, Gtiff," she says in thumb-speak.

A tall man with a beard joins us in the big square hall. "Hi, Tiff," he says, gathering some of our carrier bags and shaking my hand. He kisses Auntie Cass and turns back to me, "I'm your Uncle Dan, come on in, you must be exhausted. Let's get you a nice mug of something hot."

He leads us into a large room that has a real fire blasting out heat, making a cosy glow around the walls. Two soft, pale-blue sofas with fat cushions on them invite me to snuggle down.

"Make yourself at home, Tiff," says Auntie Cass, heading for the kitchen next door. "I'll bring in some drinks and a snack then we'll give you a guided tour of the place."

I take off my shoes and curl up on the sofa that's closest to the fire. I watch the flames dancing on the logs, chasing each other, twirling around. They start off as tiny blue sparks but quickly grow into big golden glows, making patterns and shapes that flicker shadows across the floor. I look around. One wall is completely covered in books and there's a scruffy wooden chest with an old fashioned TV balanced on top and a tatty old stereo with piles of CDs and DVDs making a tall tower. There are faded, old pink rugs covering the wooden floor and some fluffy sheepskin ones piled up in front of the fire. Everything here is old. My mum would hate it. Nothing's new. Nothing's shiny. Except for one thing.

Out of the corner of my eye a small, silver picture frame keeps glinting in the fiery glow. I drag myself from the sofa to take a look. In the frame is a picture of two girls on ponies. One has white-blonde hair and looks just like me, and the other has long, dark curls. I carefully pick up the frame and peer at it more closely. My eyes want to burrow right into the picture in the hope that it will come alive. I want to hear what the girls are chatting about, to know what they're doing. I stroke the blonde hair. I've never seen a photo of my mum when she was small. I've never even been able to imagine what she was like or what her life was like. I've only ever known my mum how she is now. Always trying harder and harder to look perfect. But in this picture she looks so beautiful because her shine is coming from the inside, lighting her face, twinkling in her eyes. She's smiling and shining brightly even though she's wearing smelly wellies that are covered in mud. And I wonder whatever could have happened to her to make her shine just disappear?

"Oh, you found the photo," says Auntie Cass, bringing in a tray of food and drinks. "Look at us, we were so sweet, and so happy. I've got loads more photos to show you, Tiff, hundreds of them. Let's spend the weekend going through them, shall we? There's so much you don't know."

While we're eating our snacks Auntie Cass tells me the story of my mum's life. She was born in Essex, near London. And when she was eight years old and Auntie Cass was twelve, their mum and dad decided to sell up and move to Sark to run a hotel. Apparently, my mum loved ponies and old films and chocolate and making shows and plays and dances for everyone to come and see. Then she became a teenager and started hanging out with a bad crowd on Guernsey, and then one day, without warning, she ran away.

"It was like she just disappeared," sighs Auntie Cass. "We all searched so hard for ages and ages. Then we had a couple of calls from her saying she was never coming back and that was that. We didn't know where she was, so there was nothing we could do. A few years later Mum and Dad decided that they just couldn't stay here any more; the place was too full of memories. So they bought a place in Spain and moved there. I never gave up though, Tiff. That's why I stayed on and took over the hotel. I've been waiting and waiting ever since." Her voice cracks and she starts to cry. "Then when your mum phoned from the police station, I just couldn't believe it. It was like talking to a ghost from the past. I was so happy. I just hopped on the first ferry I could get and raced like mad to see her." She blows her nose and strokes my cheek. "I'm just so happy you're both safe, Tiff, so happy you're here."

A little worry lump grows in my throat and my eyes start brimming over. "Why did she run away?" I ask, "Why did she do that to you all?" Guilty feelings start gnawing away in my tummy. It's stupid; *I'm* feeling guilty for what *she's* done and yet I hadn't even been born when all of this happened. "I hate her even more now," I spit. "How could she have done that to you? It's typical: Mandy's right, she just does what she wants all the time and never really cares about other people's feelings."

"Don't be too harsh on her," says Auntie Cass. "She

92

was only seventeen. I know something bad happened between her and Mandy, but we never really got to the bottom of it. Mandy just stayed quiet and turned in on herself. . . and then Holly came along."

"So that's why Mandy hates me?"

"She doesn't hate *you*, Tiff, she's just bitter."

"And your mum and dad in Spain, they're my grandparents?"

"Of course, and they're flying over from Spain to visit your mum today. They're so happy she's OK, even though she's in this mess. And they're coming to meet you at Christmas. They're so excited. But just to warn you, Tiff, they're not like your traditional grandparents," she laughs. "They're loud and boisterous like your mum. Always getting themselves into mischief."

"Come on girls, that's enough chat for now," says Uncle Dan. "Let's have the grand tour. I don't know what your favourite colour is, but I've spent the past couple of days decorating your mum's old bedroom for you. I thought you might like to wake up in the morning and look out of the same window that she did when she was twelve. To see the same view."

And I can't pretend that he isn't a little bit right.

Chapter 16

It's white...

First they show me the hotel. It's right opposite the house with a courtyard in between. It has seven bedrooms with big beds that have little heart-shaped chocolates waiting on the pillows, as welcome treats for the guests. The dining rooms have square tables with crisp white tablecloths and napkins and sparkly cutlery. The bar is cosy with red velvet-covered benches, a roaring fire and a stone floor. There are shelves and shelves of twinkling glasses and bottles, and big brass levers to pump the beer.

"Once you're settled," says Uncle Dan, "you can help out a bit if you like, to earn yourself some pocket money."

I nod. I'd like to have some money of my own that

I've earned. I'm never going to be like my mum. I'm never going to steal anything.

We wander around the gardens and they show me the rope swing and the horse carriage that the kids can play on. The air smells fresh and clean and I fill my lungs. When we come to an old derelict barn, Uncle Dan lovingly pats its walls. "You never know, Tiff, when this is all over, we might be able to make the barn into a new home for you and your mum. If we can persuade her to come home and live on Sark."

All the colour drains from my face. I am *not* living in an old ruin like this. It doesn't even have a roof! My mum would hate it; she likes the bright lights of London, we both do! She would be running off again in no time at all.

"Don't panic, Tiff," says Auntie Cass, "it's just an idea. We're going to do it up anyway, convert it into a holiday cottage." Her eyes glisten with tears. "I just really want her to come home, Tiff, to live here again, with all of us together. We thought you might like to help us with the plans?"

I peer inside the dark barn. It's full of old broken stuff and empty bottles and cobwebs that drape and dangle from beam to beam. My mind doesn't have the imagination to be able to turn this crummy old barn into a shiny new home. And anyway it's just my Auntie Cass going off on some fantasy thing about us being here forever and playing happy families with my mum.

"Don't bother doing it for us," I snap, "my mum would hate it. She's never coming back here and I'm not staying for long. As soon as she's home, I'm going straight back to London; so don't get your hopes up."

My words punch their faces and we wander on in silence as they show me round the part of the hotel that they live in; that *I* now live in. It's all friendly and light and homely. In the kitchen, Indigo is hopping about sprinkling magic with her wand. I wish she could sprinkle some on me. There's a huge farmhousey table in the middle of the room covered in Indigo's sparkly stickers and painting things, and along one wall is a massive cooker with socks and pants hung above it to dry.

Chunky old stairs take us up to the bathroom, which has an enormous old bath with painted feet and a massive shower that looms overhead. Auntie Cass and Uncle Dan's room has a four-poster style bed with swishy curtains draped down the sides, which I find a bit spooky. But Indigo's room is cheerful and bright and has a teeny wooden bed with a red patchwork quilt and a neat row of teddies, all tucked in. Finally we come to a closed wooden door.

"Shut your eyes, Tiff," says Uncle Dan, "it's a surprise."

My brain is dancing around, terrified that I might hate it, petrified that he might have done it all babyish and stupid. He opens the door and Auntie Cass gasps, her mouth drops open like a goldfish.

"It's perfect," she sighs, her eyes brimming over with tears, "Dan you've done brilliantly. What d'you think, Tiff?"

"It's white," I say, flopping on to the bed.

"Come on, Tiff," says Auntie Cass sitting next to me, "it's great. How about a 'Thank you, Uncle Dan'?"

I mimic her voice, "Thank you, Uncle Dan."

Auntie Cass looks crushed, like I've tipped a truckload of nastiness on her head. Uncle Dan comes to her rescue.

"Come on Cass," he soothes, "let's leave Tiff to settle in shall we?"

They close the door and leave me alone. I flop down on my big white bed, eat the little chocolate that's waiting on my pillow and look around. My uncle is weird. He's painted everything white. All the walls, floorboards and a chest of drawers that's tucked between one wall and the chimney breast, and a chair and a desk under the window that looks out across the woods. There are floaty white curtains, a fluffy white rug and a bedside table with a white paper lamp. My uncle Dan obviously has about as much imagination as a mushroom. Wherever did he get the idea that white was nice?

My old room in London was multicoloured with loads of fairy lights and posters and massive gold and silver cushions and a big purple egg-chair that hung from the ceiling. It was cool and full to the brim with stuff and I never had to clean it up. Chelsea's dad was always on at her about cleaning up her room, but my mum said that my room was my business. This room is boring with a capital B. Plain and white.

I feel even more like a big black smudge now. Mandy's harsh words still sting and dig away at me, niggling because I don't understand what she means. My mum and her stupid crazy life stick to me like thick black oil, creeping on to me. And I'm boiling-mad inside because what she's done is not my fault, it isn't even anything to do with me and yet I'm the one left here alone and I want to get her back for hurting me, for ruining our lives. An idea creeps into my head.

First I find some nail-varnish remover in the bathroom and rub away Miguel's stupid pink manicure. Then I scrub my teeth with fresh mint toothpaste until my whole mouth is fresh and clean. I lock the bathroom door, have a quick shower and start searching in the bathroom cupboard drawers.

The large scissors wink at me, daring me. I know my mum will go mad, but right now I don't care. I brush my long hair smooth. It falls almost to my waist. I bend right over and gather it up into a ponytail. Then I take a deep breath and chop. My ponytail flops in my hand and the rest of my hair falls all raggedy around my shoulders. I panic a bit and try to straighten it up, but I just make things worse. It looks terrible. What have I done? I stare into the mirror and the new me with crazy, raggedy hair stares right back.

I'm not my mum. And she's not me. Whatever she's done is nothing to do with me. I have to keep on remembering that. *Huh!* I think, dressing myself in my new clothes. Who's scared of meeting new kids and having a new life? Who's scared of being away from her mum and all alone? Not me.

Chapter 17

Go girl...

Auntie Cass gasps when she sees what I've done to my hair, but she doesn't burrow away with questions, I think she understands.

"Do you want me to straighten it up for you?" she smiles. "Tiffany Morris, you are so like your mum. That's exactly the sort of thing she would do at your age. I bet she'll go crazy when she finds out."

I shrug because I don't care what my mum thinks. But I do need Auntie Cass's help. I can't start my new school looking like a freak so I sit still while she patiently chops away at the crooked ends. When she's finished I look in the mirror and see a whole new me.

And I love it! A little tiny bubble of happiness peeps out of my heart.

Suppertime is different here. For one thing we all sit around the big table instead of in front of the TV. And it's a no-junk-food zone. The pizza Auntie Cass took me for must have been a pity-treat because the kitchen here is full of vegetables, vegetables and more vegetables. I have never seen so many. Only homemade things are allowed and everything is made from scratch. My tummy is longing for a takeaway burger and chips and a supersize chocolate milkshake. Or a bucket of chicken and a Coke-float.

Indigo drags her chair close to mine and peers at me, smiling. She's happily tucking into a big mound of steamy green veg. I hate green veg, and the sight of it all piled high on my plate makes me want to vomit all over the table. I wish I had the guts to do it, just to see what old joke Uncle Dan would come up with to cover up the fact that I'm starting to get on his nerves. But I don't. I just push the food around my plate and make a lot of clinking noise with my cutlery.

After dinner I go up to my room to unpack. Auntie Cass knocks and peeps her head around my door, "Are you OK, sweetheart?" she asks, "is there anything you need?"

"No," I say, yawning.

"I think it's probably bedtime now," she says, ruffling my hair. "What time do you usually go to bed?"

"Whenever," I say. "It depends what we're doing."

"Well I think nine o'clock is a good time here."

"Nine!" I shriek. "You must be joking!"

"Not joking," she says. "Let's try it out and see how it goes. I think once you get into the routine of school and cycling around all day, you'll find that you're ready for bed by nine."

Nine is ultra-early for bedtime. In my old life my mum and I would probably be getting ready to go out for food or we'd be ordering a takeaway and checking if there's anything good on TV. But Auntie Cass is not my mum, obviously. And anyway, I'm going to be mega bored because I don't actually have many things to do here, and no one seems to watch much TV in this house.

"Do you want to talk, Tiff?" she asks.

"No, there's nothing to talk about."

"Well, I just want to say that you're really welcome here. I know it feels difficult right now, but you'll get used to things, I promise. Here," she says, putting a picture of me and my mum on my bedside table. "I hope you don't mind, but I brought this from your house, I thought you might like it."

The photo starts me thinking about my mum again. I stare at it for ages after Auntie Cass has gone. It's one of my mum and me on the beach last year, hugging and laughing. I gaze at her familiar face, hating her stupid false smile and her big stolen sunglasses that she's pushed right back on the top of her head. I feel like I don't even know her any more. Half of me wants to throw her out of the window or smash her against the wall and the other half wants to run to her and hug her and breathe in her perfume smell. My tummy does an annoying little flip and a burst of love peeps its head out from my heart. I quickly kiss her cheek goodnight, and then turn the picture to face the wall to punish her for breaking us apart. Then, for the first time since last Friday night, I drift into a deep, deep sleep.

In the morning Indigo puts on her new fairy wings and cycles off to school on her own. Auntie Cass notices the worry on my face.

"It's OK, there's no danger here, Tiff, even the little ones make their own way to school. The kids whizz about all over the place, you just have to listen for the tractors and you can hear them coming! You'll soon get the hang of it. Uncle Dan will take you to buy a bike and then you can have a go yourself." She gives me a big hug and kisses the top of my head. I shrug her off.

"I told you already, I don't want one."

Uncle Dan gets up and shuffles around the kitchen. "We're going to get you one anyway, Tiff. Like it or not."

"You can't make me," I hiss. "You're not my dad."

"Obviously not," he says. "But that doesn't mean I can't spoil you. Now, go and get your coat on. We're going shopping."

Choosing the bike is the easy bit. I choose a red one that has a basket on the front, and twelve gears. Learning to ride the bike is a bit more complicated. Uncle Dan holds on to the back of the saddle, helping me keep my balance, but still I wobble along like a stupid baby. Indigo is only five years old and a million times better than me already. We gently speed up until Uncle Dan's running along beside me, still holding on. I grip on to the handlebars, trying to keep the wheel going in a straight line. We go faster and faster until he suddenly lets go. The cold wind blows through my new hair and nips my fingers and nose. I'm flying with the wind, blowing in the breeze.

"You're doing it, Tiff, you're a natural," he calls.

But then the wheel skids on a tiny stone. I lose control and feel myself skidding and sliding towards the floor. Bump! I land with a massive thud on the ground. My new jeans are all scuffed, my shoulder's sore and my face is glowing red. I feel stupid, stupid, stupid and never want to try again. Uncle Dan comes to the rescue and gives me a warm bear hug.

"You're brilliant, Tiff," he reassures. "Next try and you'll be off."

But I don't want to try again. Tiny tears squeeze out of my eyes. I sniff them away.

"Forget it," I sniff, kicking a stone. "I'm never trying that again. I'll walk."

"Oh, come on Tiff, lighten up, will you?"

"You try having your whole entire life ruined," I shout, "then see how you cope." I start to stomp off.

"I'm sorry, Tiff," he puffs, running to catch me up. "I know this isn't easy for you, but it's not my fault is it? I'm just trying to help."

He guides me back to the bike. "Now the first rule of riding a bike," he says, "or horse, for that matter, is that if you fall off you must get straight back on. Otherwise you'll lose your confidence for good. It's OK, I'm here with you."

"But I look stupid," I say, "like a baby, I can't even do it right. Why didn't my mum teach me all this stuff when I was small, when you're supposed to?"

"I don't know, Tiff," he says, picking up my bike and handing it back to me, "but I do know that right now you've got a choice. You can either give up and carry on moaning about how things haven't gone right for you, or you can get back on and learn something new."

My shaky legs get back on. Uncle Dan holds tight to the saddle again and off we go. I practise turning the wheel a little to regain my balance each time I lose it and find that the more I relax the easier it becomes. We go faster and faster and the wind blows through my hair. Uncle Dan gives a gentle push and I'm off. I start pedalling like mad, keeping my balance and watching for stones. The houses and trees fly past me getting faster and faster. And suddenly I'm doing it all on my own. Uncle Dan runs to catch up with me.

"Go girl," he shouts into the wind. "Go girl."

Chapter 18

Hands off, Tiffany...

I start my new school on Friday morning and can't believe so much has happened in my life in just one week. It's like I don't even know myself any more. Last Friday I went off to a school that had over one thousand kids in it. Now I'm riding *a bike* to a school where there are only fifty-seven pupils!

We're divided into three classrooms, with mixed age-groups in each class. I'm put in Class 3, which is for Years 6, 7, 8 and 9. There are only two other Year 7 kids apart from me: a girl called Isla and a boy called Max and I'm going to be sitting on a table with them. My new teacher, Mrs Davies, introduces me to the class and both Isla and Max give me a welcome smile, even though I must look like the crazy-red-face new girl.

"I want you to have a go at writing a poem about Christmas," says Mrs Davies. "And I want you to think a little deeper than the usual presents, trees and carol concerts. Think about what Christmas really means to you. For some people it's a happy time, but for others it can be sad or lonely. See what you can come up with."

With all the changes going on in my life I'd forgotten that Christmas was only one month away. A little panic starts up in my head. I've only ever spent Christmas with my mum, and we always book ourselves into some flash hotel with a pool and a spa. Mum always goes crazy with her credit cards and I always get busy making Christmassy things and hanging them all around our room, making it twinkle and shine. I always thought they were the best Christmases ever, but that's all over now. Thanks to *her*.

I draw little squiggles and swirls and baby snowmen all around my page, but have trouble finding poemy words. Worry bugs start scratching around my brain. Will my mum be home for Christmas or not? I don't want her here, but how will it be with Auntie Cass and Uncle Dan and Indigo? And what about meeting my grandparents? My heart squeezes tight and makes a familiar little lump arrive in my throat. I try to swallow it down but it keeps on popping up, pushing tears into my eyes. I blink a lot to push them away. I must not let myself cry here. As much as I hate my mum and never want to see her again, the thought of not being with her for Christmas feels scary.

Isla looks at me, and smiles. She's written a really long poem already and decorated her paper with mini Christmas trees all around the edge. "Are you OK, Tiff?" she asks.

I roll my eyes at her and yawn. "I'm just tired," I lie. "And I can't believe you haven't all died of boredom being at this school. . . it's like a school for babies. Not like my school in London."

Isla's eyes grow huge and sparkle. "Are you from London?" she says. "That's so cool. What's it like?"

"It's brilliant. There's loads of amazing stuff going on all the time," I say. "I'm only staying in this dump with my auntie while my mum's away working, I'll be going back to London as soon as she's finished. The countryside sucks."

Isla's face drops and I feel mean. But it's too late to go back now.

"Oh," she says. "Well, I like it here. It's peaceful and there's loads to do, you know."

I can tell that she's trying to be friendly but it's hard to be friendly back. I sort of try.

"Like what?" I ask.

"Well, we all go riding after school and at the weekends. Have you got a pony?" she says, adding some snowflakes to her poem.

I shake my head, thinking that I must be the only girl in the entire world who had a dog just for one day.

"Shame," she says. "Still there's other stuff you can join in with."

I shrug, but inside I am wondering if she's right.

At break time everyone charges downstairs on to the grass outside. I follow slowly behind, but Max and Isla are waiting for me, zipped up against the chilly wind.

"Hi," says Max. "So you're from London. I went to London Zoo once, to the insect house."

"You're just weird, Max," Isla says, rolling her eyes, "too weird for words." Then she looks at me.

"He collects insects, you know, and keeps them in hundreds of jars in his tree house. Spooky if you ask me."

Just then, my heart sinks as Mandy's daughter Holly comes over.

"Hi Holly," says Isla, "d'you want to join us?"

Holly wrinkles her nose. "Er, no! There's bad smell here today and it's lingering in that direction," she says, pointing at me. "And anyway, did you forget about our *secret* plan?" She whispers into Isla's ear and they both fall about giggling.

"Bye bye, Tiffany Morris," Holly says in a sour voice, pulling Isla away. "And Max, you freak! Found any amazing spiders lately? Make sure you don't get bitten, you might turn into Spider-Man!"

"Yeah, right," says Max. "Then at least then I could wipe out losers like you."

"Takes one to know one," Holly retaliates.

Even though I was pretty mean to Isla and Max earlier, I can't stand Holly and I want to tell her exactly what I think of her and her mum. But before I get the chance to say anything, she is dragging Isla away.

"Sorry, Tiff," says Isla, leaving me alone with Max. "See you after break."

"What's her problem?" I ask Max. "I haven't even said a word to her yet and she's got something major against me."

"She's just Holly," he says. "She's got something against everyone. Her and Isla have been best friends since Isla came to the island. And Holly gets jealous if anyone else gets too close."

"Yeah, well, she doesn't have to worry about me, I'll be off back to London soon. I don't need to make friends here," I lie, "I've got plenty of my own *normal* friends back home."

Suddenly I feel all lost and empty, like a little ship rowing itself into a big sea, and secretly looking for something to tie itself on to. I wish my ruby slippers were real, like Dorothy's, so I could click my heels and magic myself back home. Why am I being so mean to this weird insect-loving boy?

"I'm not that weird you know," says Max, reading my thoughts. "Holly's way more weird than me. I just love wildlife and drawing and stuff. And anyway, I can't see that there's a law against that."

In maths, Mrs Davies invites Holly to sit at our table, because although she's in the year above us, she needs extra help because it's not her best subject.

"So," she smirks, snuggling closer to Isla, "we all know about you, Tiffany Morris."

My tummy ties itself in knots. "You probably do," I brave, "I'm staying with my Auntie Cass, at the Hotel Roche Noir, while my mum's away working."

"I know," she says with a sour smile. "It's a small island, Tiffany, which means that everyone knows everyone else's business. Only six hundred people live on Sark, and it's only three miles long, so a new person stands out like a lighthouse. And then the gossip flies around. You'll see." She pulls her pencil case, ruler and water bottle out of her bag and puts them on the table in front of her. Then she looks at me, licks her finger and draws a wet circle on the desktop around her things.

"Hands off, Tiffany Morris," she says, shooting me with her eyes, "which means no touching. Get my drift?"

I glare back at her, staring her out, trying to stay brave. But inside I'm panicking and crumbling. What does she know? She can't have heard that Mum's in prison. We haven't told anyone! I keep on staring, holding my fear together and she keeps on staring back. She's good, but not as good as Matilda and not as good as me. Finally, her green eyes flick away. She pokes her tongue out at me, huffs and gets back to her worksheet. I imagine licking my finger and writing a number one in the air. One point to me, Holly Hutchinson!

Chapter 19

Hi, babe...

Everyone on Sark goes home for lunch, and when me and Indigo get back, Auntie Cass hands me a white envelope with "HMP Henmoore" stamped across the top. I know it's from my mum. My heart sinks. I stare at the letter, not wanting to open it, in fact not wanting it, full stop. My washing-machine tummy starts spinning again and although I try hard to eat my lunch, I just pick at it because my appetite has run away. I wish I could run away too, but I'm stuck here like my mum was on this stupid little island, and anyway, I have nowhere to run to. It's like I'm in prison as well, with the sea keeping me in, instead of walls and locked doors.

I want Chelsea. She'd know what to do. She'd know how to make me laugh and forget my troubles. But all I have is weird Max, spiteful Holly and Isla who seems friendly enough, but is somehow locked under Holly's spell. Auntie Cass gives me a hug. I push her away. "Are you going to open it," she teases, "or keep it as an ornament?"

I take the envelope and without thinking I tear it in half. Auntie Cass gasps. I gasp because even I am shocked by what I've done. Why can't she just leave me alone? I pick up the pieces and run to my room.

"Tiff," calls Auntie Cass, running after me.

"Just leave me alone," I shout. "Please, will all of you just leave me alone!"

I slam my bedroom door, grab the photo of me and mum and throw it against the wall. The glass smashes and the frame makes a black mark on the white wall. "I hate you, I hate you, I hate you!" I scream. Then I pick up the torn letter and tear it into little pieces until it's paper confetti falling to the floor. Auntie Cass runs in, pulls me into her arms and will not let me go. I push and kick and scream, but she keeps on holding me tighter and tighter until I almost can't breathe.

"Leave me alone!" I scream. "I don't want you; I don't want anyone."

"Hey," she soothes, collapsing us both on the bed and holding me in her arms, "I know you're angry with your mum, Tiff, but I don't think all this raging at the rest of the world is helping, do you?"

I sniff back the tears that are sneaking through and shrug.

"In case you hadn't noticed we're on your side, Tiff; we're here to support you through this. We love you."

Her words move through my body like cold soup. There's no way I'm trusting anyone to love me ever again, not ever! I'm much better off taking care of myself. I free my body from her grip, run downstairs, grab my bike and race back to the stupid little school.

Later, when I get home from school, I slide into the house and head straight to my room. The smashed picture is magically mended and back in its place. I take a look at the girl smiling out from the photo and find it hard to believe it's me. I look so happy. But that was before I knew mum's stealing had ruined my life. Looking at my smile, I realise it wasn't only things and money my mum stole, but happiness too, my happiness and her own. I turn the picture back to face the wall. Someone has also magically pieced together the tiny bits of letter confetti, stuck them together with tape and laid it on my bed. I don't want to read it but my eyes are curious.

Finally, I open the chocolate that's been left on my pillow and settle down to read. I can always rip it up again afterwards.

Hi, babe,

So, at last you've landed on Sark and met some of your family! Do you think it's the most boring place in the world? Cass and Dan are all right, but as for the rest of them, B.O.R.I.N.G! Still, it was a good idea of yours to call Cass. She was over the moon to hear about you and way better than that foster place I imagine. I should be out of this dump in a flish of a flash, Tiff. I have this great solicitor working for me, so fingers crossed I'll come and rescue you soon. Then we'll be back in the bright lights, babe, where we belong. It was all Mikey's fault, Tiff, nothing to do with me.

I'm sharing my room with three other girls. Two of them are great and we're having a right giggle, but the other one's a bit of a nutter so we stay well clear.

I'm allowed to do 'Education' here and don't laugh, but I've taken up cooking. The queen of fast food is learning to chop onions. When I'm out of here I'll cook you a celebration feast. I'm gagging for a burger, though, and a glass of vino. Shame you can't come and visit me and smuggle some in, ha ha! Why don't you want to speak on the phone?

I love you, babe,

You and me, babe. You and me,

Love Mama xxxxxxxxxxxxxxxx

Chapter 20

Henmoore Prison...

A whole week has passed and I still haven't written back to my mum. Auntie Cass is putting major pressure on me.

"Just write and tell her what you've been up to," she says. "She must be missing you loads, Tiff, and wondering how you are."

"She should have thought of that first," I spit, "before she got herself into all this trouble and wrote me the most stupid letter ever in the world. It's like I've just popped to the shops or something. She didn't even ask how I was. She's pathetic!"

"I know, sweetheart, it's hard, but sometimes we

do things without thinking and then it's not until afterwards that we realise the hurt we've caused."

"But she still doesn't realise that she's done anything wrong," I say. "She didn't even say sorry in her letter, she just went on about having a laugh and learning to cook."

"Just have a go," she sighs, handing me a freshly baked chocolate brownie. "Do your best."

I take a second chocolate brownie up to my room and some special notepaper that has the name of the hotel on the top, with a little picture of a black rock in the corner. The page is staring at me waiting for words, but I don't even know where to start. I'd quite like to begin the letter with something like, *Dear Mum, Thanks for ruining my life*, or *Dear Mum, I'm glad you're having a nice time without me.* Or maybe, *Dear Mum, how could you be so selfish and hurt your family so much by running away and then hurt me by being so stupid?* But I don't think that's the kind of letter that Auntie Cass has in mind.

It's already ten thirty and I'm supposed to be meeting Isla and Max in his dumb tree house at eleven, so I don't have a lot of time left. Chelsea would laugh at me if she could see the kind of people I hang out with now, but I don't have a lot of choice, do I? It's either hanging

122

out with them, or sitting on my own in a boring white room with no TV. It sounds like my mum is having a better time in prison. I pick up my pen, take a deep breath and begin.

Dear Mum,

I'm sitting at a little desk in the bedroom that you used to have when you were my age. Uncle Dan painted the whole room boring white for me and left me a mini chocolate on my pillow. It's so bright it makes my eyes go funny. School is so lame. It's a school for babies, which means I'm not learning anything at all. Which is fine by me. I know what you've done, Mum. I know our life was a lie. I have two boring friends. I have to hang out with them because there's nothing else to do. Isla has a pony and Max's family has loads of horses, but he likes insects and drawing. I have one enemy called Holly. In fact I have two enemies. Her mum, Mandy, doesn't like me either. Or you. What did you do to her, Mum? Well, whatever it was she's still pretty angry about it all. I have a cousin who is five and she's called Indigo, she likes it when I paint her nails pink for her. I've stopped painting my nails. Soon I'm going to be in a dumb school concert and I have to read a poem and you'll miss it. I have a red bike and have to wear pathetic wellies because it rains so much. Why didn't you ever teach me how to ride a bike? It's stupid. I'm earning my own money by collecting glasses and cleaning tables in the bar for Uncle Dan, which means I have to put up with his jokes.

Anyway, bye then.

From Tiffany x

It's a stupid letter but I don't care. I'm more worried about getting the letter safely in the letterbox without anyone seeing it's addressed to a prison, than what's in the actual letter itself. I stuff it in the envelope and call goodbye to Auntie Cass. When I'm on my bike I zip it safely in my jacket pocket and speed off toward the post office. I need a stamp, so I have to go inside and buy one.

"I need a stamp for a letter to England," I say.

"Give it here, pet," says the post office lady, "I'll stick it on for you and pop it in the sack."

"Er, no, it's all right, I'll just take the stamp and,

er, these." I say picking up three chocolate bars and thrusting some money into her hand. My heart is thumping in my chest. I mustn't let her see the letter.

"Suit yourself, pet," she says, handing me my change.

Back outside, I hide behind the large blue postbox, away from the Saturday shoppers, and shove the stamp on the right hand corner of the envelope. It feels like I have a bomb in my hand that's waiting to explode. My face is hot, my hands are shaking and I feel all guilty, like I've done something wrong. I want to get rid of it quick so I take a good look around to make sure no one's looking and dart round to the front of the postbox. Just as I'm about to throw the letter into its mouth, the door of the shop opposite opens wide and Holly steps outside.

"Ah, it's Tiffany Morris. Writing a love letter are we?" she sneers.

"Er, no." My letter is trembling in midair. I feel like all the oxygen has been sucked from my lungs and my legs have turned to jelly.

"Yes it is! It's a love letter. How *sweet*. What's your boyfriend's name?" She's coming close.

I can't speak and I'm willing my hand to put the letter in the box.

"Well, let's have a look at it then, maybe I would like to have his address so I can write too!" she sneers. Then before I can stop her she's snatched the letter from my hand and is staring at the address.

"No way!" she shrieks. "Carla Morris is *in prison*! *Just* as my mum predicted," she spits, "she's in big trouble again."

All of a sudden, my strength comes back. "Give it to me," I hiss. "It's none of your business." I snatch the letter back and throw it in the postbox. "I don't know what happened between your mum and mine but it's nothing to do with us."

"I disagree, Tiffany Morris, it appears it has *everything* to do with us. And if we really want to keep this little secret between ourselves I think maybe we'll start with my maths homework. What do you reckon?"

I can see that I'm cornered. How can this be happening? Everything will be even worse if the whole of Sark finds out my mum's a criminal!

"I'll do it," I say quietly. "Just don't tell anyone, OK. Please?"

Chapter 21

Grown-ups make mistakes too. . .

I head off to the tree house to meet Max and Isla and hope they'll be able to take my mind off Holly. Despite the fact I've hardly been friendly since I arrived, Max and Isla seem to like me for some weird reason. I hand everyone a chocolate bar, as a kind of peace offering, my hands still trembling. I hope the sugar might calm me down. Holly is evil, but worse than that, I'm furious with myself for getting caught out. I'm stupid. Why didn't I ask Auntie Cass to post it for me, or why couldn't I have been more careful, like a normal person? I just stood there like a dummy, frozen to the spot, virtually waiting for

Holly to take the letter from me. I might as well have wrapped it up in sparkly paper and ribbons and popped it through her letter box so she could read the whole thing. I'd like to tell someone what happened, but I can't.

Instead I ask Max and Isla if either of them know anything about what happened between my mum and Mandy years ago. The whole thing is bugging me and I just need to know the truth. I need to get to the bottom of it and try to sort it out. Otherwise I'll be doing Holly's homework for the rest of my life, and she might not stop there. But they just shrug their shoulders and shake their heads. Max says his mum isn't into island gossip.

"My mum's not interested in anything," he says, "unless it's a horse. And that includes me. I sometimes think it would've been better if I'd been born with four legs and a mane."

Isla says her family has only been on the island for the past six years so they hadn't even heard of my mum and me before I arrived.

"I did ask Holly," she says, "but she wouldn't tell. She told me not to get involved. And anyway, I've got my own problems to be worrying about. My parents have just told me that they want me to go to boarding school back in England next year. They've got it all planned out."

"Why do they want to send you off?" I ask, forgetting my own troubles for a moment.

"They think our school is too small," she says, "and lots of kids go off-island to do GCSEs and things. But I don't want to go," she sniffs. "I like it here. And anyway you can get GCSEs here, it's not impossible."

"Why are you worrying about GCSEs?" I ask. "We're only twelve. We haven't got exams and stuff like that to worry about for years. This place is so weird."

Max is busy with his sketchbook drawing an army of disgusting stick insects. "She's right you know, Isla, why can't you just tell them?" he says. "Just say you like it here and you don't want to go. It's your life."

"Yeah, right," she sighs, "like they'll listen to me! I always have to go along with what they want. I suppose I don't want to upset them or disappoint them or something."

"Well, you can't be as much of a disappointment to your parents as I am to mine," Max says. "My dad has great plans for me being some kind of zoologist or something, but I'm too stupid, I have trouble even reading a whole book. I'd be no use at a smart school. I'm better off sticking to my drawing."

"I didn't know you have trouble reading," I say. "You should get tested for dyslexia, Max. My best friend Chelsea's dyslexic, but it doesn't mean she's stupid. She's got a really high IQ. Why don't you get tested?"

"Nah," he says, "sounds like too much trouble to me."

I turn to Isla. "I've had enough of grown-ups always telling me what to do all the time. And it's not as if they always get it right, anyway. Grown-ups make mistakes too. I'm just going to do what I want from now on. You should too."

"Hm," says Isla, but she doesn't look convinced. "Anyway, I have to go now. I promised I'd meet Holly and go for a ride."

I leave Max to his drawing and while Isla and Holly are out horse riding I get busy doing two lots of maths homework. The first bit of Holly's grand plan is that I work out all the answers on the sheet then give her a copy so she can fill it in in her own writing. The second bit is that I have to make a couple of mistakes on my sheet so Mrs Davies won't get suspicious. It's rubbish.

My marks are going to dive downhill, but I don't exactly have a choice, do I?

I sneak out of the house just before bedtime to meet Holly in the lane. The moon is only a tiny sliver in the sky, and my torch makes dark shadows hang in the trees.

"Well done, Tiffany," she sneers. "And I've been thinking about that boring Christmas project we have to do. I'm so tired I was wondering if you'd like to do it for me?"

"No way," I say. "Nothing else."

"Shame," she threatens. "Well, if you're only going to do the maths then I won't be able to guarantee that certain important addresses and certain important information about your precious mother don't get shared around the island, will I?"

My fists curl and my teeth grind against each other. And even though I want to push her into a dark corner in the shadows and make her feel scared, I somehow find myself agreeing to her plan. I feel like my prison walls are growing taller and thicker all around me. Holly is the warden who is holding the key, and I'm the prisoner left feeling helpless and alone.

Chapter 22

Sure you've remembered to pay. . .?

It's nearly Christmas. Last week we did our school carol-concert and I had to stand up and read out my poem in front of everyone. I felt like a kid at primary school again. The whole thing was ridiculous. Max had to sing a solo and Isla and Holly played a recorder duet of "Away in a Manger". Uncle Dan recorded the whole cheesy thing on his camcorder and says we have to send it to Mum as part of her Christmas present. I think it's a stupid idea. She won't be interested in watching me, anyway. In my London school she always arrived at things like concerts and parents' evenings at least half an hour late. She said it was important to make a good entrance, to get noticed. She got noticed, all right, but not because she looked great, more because she was always such a mess. She'd clip clop noisily in on her stupid pointy heels, smelling of wine and make too-loud 'shushing' noises while she was trying to find her seat in the dark. She was so embarrassing. But Uncle Dan and Auntie Cass were completely well-behaved. They arrived early to get the best seats and didn't make a fuss.

Indigo is mega-hyped about Christmas. She's taken to wearing a Santa hat most of the time and nearly burst with excitement when the real Santa came to visit us at school. Yesterday we picked up our tree from the Gallery Stores and spent the evening rummaging through boxes and boxes of old decorations from the loft. Auntie Cass rooted out a couple of wobbly cotton-wool snowmen that she and Mum had made when they were small. I held them in the palm of my hand and gazed at them. My mum's hands have actually touched them, actually made them, and Auntie Cass has kept them safe. I've never had a family history before; it's always just been Mum and me.

"I don't know why you bother to hang on to those old things. Mum and I always get shiny new decorations every year. We never use the same ones twice." And I realise that I am the rubbish one who's talking rubbish. We didn't go and buy new decorations, did we? My mum just stole them somehow because she was so addicted to having shiny new things.

Today I'm going on the ferry over to Guernsey with Auntie Cass for our grand Christmas shopping expedition. Indigo's not so happy about it because she has to stay at home with Uncle Dan, who's trying to tempt her with plans for icing our Christmas cake and making mince pies. I'd quite like to join in with all that stuff too, but I'd never say and anyway, I have some shopping to do myself. I've promised Max that he can tag along with us because his mum's too busy for things like Christmas shopping. Max says his mum does all her shopping on the internet and hardly ever leaves the island, unless it's to do with horses.

The ferry to Guernsey is crammed full of Christmas shoppers, buzzing with excitement. Isla keeps on flitting backwards and forwards between sitting with us and sitting with Holly and Mandy, who are tucked in the corner at the back. Holly's eyes are boring into my back, but I don't care. I got all her maths homework and a whole Christmas project done before school broke up. Now I'm hoping she'll leave me in peace until next term.

"It's OK, Isla," I say. "You can sit with Holly if you like, I don't mind."

"Thanks," she whispers. "It's just that I'd rather sit with you two, but when I do I always end up feeling guilty. Holly and I have been best friends since I moved here and we started riding together. I feel bad leaving her and—"

"But it's her that's the problem," Max cuts in. "It's her that thinks I'm weird and that Tiff smells, or whatever stupid thing it is she keeps saying. She could just give up, be friends with us all and join in. Nobody would mind would they?"

Isla and Max look at me waiting for my answer.

"It's not as if it's anything to do with me is it? I mean, it's not as if I'm really friends with any of you." I say. "I've got my own best friend back at home. I'm not going to be hanging around here with you lot for much longer, so do what you want, I don't care."

My words sting their cheeks, but they swallow their hurt. Isla heads silently to the back of the ferry and gets all cosy with Holly. And Max turns his back to me and stares out across the sea. My heart is thumping in my chest and my spiteful words are burning my tongue.

It's the first time I've been back to Guernsey since I arrived on Sark, and I've almost forgotten what real shops are like. I feel more at home here with cars and streets and hustle and bustle. There are twinkling lights everywhere and huddles of people singing on street corners. Auntie Cass says she has some "top secret" shopping to do, so we plan to meet her for lunch in an hour and Max and I head off alone. I'm surprised he's still speaking to me after what I said on the ferry.

"What d'you need to get, Max?" I ask.

"Dunno, really," he says. "Something for my mum and dad, I guess."

"What about your brother?"

"Nah, my mum sorts all that and wraps it up, and I just have to write the label. Why are you even interested, Tiff, you know, as you're not even my friend or anything?"

And I want to say I'm sorry for my mean words and that I'd like to be his friend, really, it's just I can't let myself get close. But my apology gets stuck in my throat and a sorry silence hangs in the air.

"I'm not really interested in shopping and stuff, anyway," he says, filling the space. "I just like drawing really."

And even while we're walking along he's got his little sketchbook out and he's sketching away, drawing everything in sight.

I'm still determined to shop, though, and I treat myself to a new top, a belt and a pair of sparkly earrings. Memories of shopping with my mum float in and out of my mind. Cool memories of us trying stuff on and giggling our heads off weave in and out of the not-so-cool ones – the memories of her taking off security tags in the changing room and stuffing things in my school bag.

Once we've done most of our shopping I ask Max to wait while I buy one more present.

"I have a bit of 'top secret' shopping to do myself," I say. "I'll meet you outside the chemist in fifteen minutes?"

"Sure," he says, his head burrowed into his sketchpad, "see you in a while."

I dart into a book shop and buy Max a little book all about nature to cheer him up and to say sorry for being so horrible. It's full of pictures that he can copy with not too many difficult words to read. Then I head to my favourite accessories store to get Isla a sparkly purse. Then, just as I'm about to leave the shop, Mandy steps in my way.

"You've got a lot of things in your bags, Tiffany Morris," she spits. "Sure you've remembered to pay for it all?"

"I d-d-did," I stutter. "I did pay for it. I've got the receipts."

"Just checking," she says.

I'm getting tired of this and want to ask her once and for all what her problem is. But my bold words shrivel in my mouth and I swallow them down.

"I need to go," I mumble, pushing past. "I have to meet my auntie."

Out in the street I find Max waiting for me, still sketching away.

"I saw Mandy and she had another go at me," I say. "What is it with her?"

I wish I could tell him all about it. I wish I could tell him that my mum's in prison and that I hate her for it. And that Holly knows my secret and is bullying me. I wish I could tell him all about how I had a dog for a day and that I miss her as much as if I'd had her for a hundred years. I wish I could tell him the truth, get it off my chest, and get it out of my mind. Lying to Max doesn't feel good. It was OK at first because he was just a weird boy who I didn't care about, but now he's starting to feel like a friend.

Maybe I'll tell him soon, but right now I need something to send to my mum (Aunt Cassie insisted) and something for my grandpa and grandma.

"OK," I say to Max. "What do you buy grandparents who you've never even met?"

Before Max can answer, I have an idea. I drag him into a gift shop and we find two picture frames the exact right size for his sketchbook pages. One is mosaic, made from tiny little bits of shiny glass, and the other is wooden and plain.

"How much would you charge to draw two portraits of me?" I ask.

"Ahh, Madame," he says, with a mock French accent, "for you, I sink one milkshake at Kristina's and a batch of your 'omemade chocolate brownies would seal the deal."

"Done," I say, shaking his hand.

Chapter 23

Hello, hello, hello...

It's two days before Christmas and everything is ready. Our tree is twinkling, the big log fire is roaring away and Uncle Dan is putting the finishing touches to our special welcome-home lunch for my grandparents. My tummy feels queasy. I've never had to welcome anyone home before. Except my mum when she's been out on one of her girly nights with Bianca, and that usually involves making her some strong black coffee and settling her into bed. But this is different. This family stuff is new to me. I'm wearing my new top and belt that I bought in Guernsey and a pair of jeans that Auntie Cass got for me. I keep hopping about from one foot to the other not really knowing what to do with myself.

I try to keep Indigo busy by making some paper chains, but she's leaping about pretending to be a Christmas fairy and doesn't want to sit down. She's making me feel even more agitated. I've never had grandparents before, and I don't know what it's going to be like. I don't know if I should shake their hands and be all stuffy and polite or if they're going to be all disgusting and huggy and squish me in a big bear-hug and slobber wet kisses on my cheek. I asked Max what it's like having grandparents, but he was useless. He just said it felt normal. But I don't know what normal is any more.

"Hello, hello, hello," booms a big voice in the hallway. "Anyone at home?"

Everyone runs into the hall. Indigo is flapping about and a man with a face as brown as a chestnut, and a big gold chain hanging from his neck, scoops her up into the air and swings her around.

"Hello, my little princess," he says, "what's Grandpa got here for you then?" And he magics a cupcake from behind her ear, making her squeal and leap about in his arms. Being five looks so much easier than being twelve.

x

141

"And look at you," he says, turning to me. "Eh, Margie," he says to a tanned lady with shiny silvery hair and a million diamonds on her fingers. "Look at her, would you believe it?" And they both just stare at me. I shuffle from foot to foot and make a tiny wave with my hand.

"I'm sorry, m'darling," he says, launching me into a twirl. "Shouldn't stare at you like that. It's just I'm gobsmacked, we both are. You look the double of your mum when she was your age. What do you think Margie? Eh?"

"Oh, give her here," she says pulling me into a Grandma bear-hug. She starts patting me and stroking me and kissing me like crazy. Tears are spilling over her black-mascara eyes and running on to her rosy cheeks.

Then Grandpa wells up again, his eyes all sparkly with joy. "Would you Adam and Eve it?" he says. "I've never seen anything like it in me life. It's like you've spun us back a few years and your mum's just walked in from school. Come 'ere again," he smiles, joining in my Grandma hug. "I'm the happiest man alive."

Then tears start streaming down my cheeks too, and I don't know why, but they're happy tears, not sad tears. They're happy tears that don't need wiping away. And then we all hug together. Auntie Cass and Uncle Dan join in and Indigo squirrels her way into the middle and we all stand there hugging and breathing each other in. I can feel the love from my family seeping into my bones. It scares me. I can't trust them, can I? What if they let me down like Mum? I pull away and scowl.

"What this?" says my grandpa, ignoring my scowl and fiddling behind my ear. Then he pulls out a magic cupcake for me too and I know that I have to let my new family right into my heart.

On Christmas Eve the hotel is busy with families celebrating, and it's all hands on deck. I'm running backwards and forwards like a mad thing with dirty plates and glasses. Uncle Dan and Auntie Cass are busy in the kitchen. My grandpa and grandma are running the bar and Indigo is entertaining everyone with her Christmas fairy dance.

"Just like the old days," smiles Grandpa, bursting into song.

After midnight mass in the church, Max, Isla and

143

I huddle together and exchange our presents. Max gives me a flat parcel, with two thin bumps in the middle, wrapped in green shiny paper. And Isla gives me a squishy one wrapped in red paper with shiny silver bows. I give them their presents, which are wrapped in snowman paper with red sparkly ties. Holly's green eyes hover on the edge of our little group, sending jealous poison arrows through the air. Isla hops over and gives her a present too, and I see Holly smile and think how much prettier she looks when she's happy.

After everyone's wished everyone a merry Christmas I troop home with my family under a black and starry sky. Indigo fell asleep ages ago and is snoozing soundly in Uncle Dan's arms, and Auntie Cass has a sleepy, faraway look on her face that reminds me of my mum. I'm in the middle of my very own grandpa and grandma who are holding on to me tightly, like they never want to let me go.

"Look at the stars, Tiffany," Grandpa says. "Special Sarkian stars, like twinkling stardust, falling into your eyes."

I look up, and a million twinkling stars are falling on me like silver rain kissing my face.

"Do you know, Tiff," he smiles, "I think you're the best Christmas present an old man like me could ever wish for."

I don't want to push his kind words away but it's still so hard.

"I know this is all very difficult for you, babe," he says. "I know your mum's hurt you a lot and you're probably feeling angry and scared and all alone in the world. But I need to tell you that you're not, Tiff. You've got us now, and I promise you're never gonna be left alone again. Your Auntie Cass and Uncle Dan are doing their best, babe. You've gotta give 'em a chance. Know what I mean?"

I nod.

"And your mum's not all bad, is she? She might not be perfect, and she's certainly got herself into a big pickle this time, but she does love you, Tiff, I'm sure of that."

Tiny little star tears slip on to my cheeks because I know what he's saying is true.

"You're part of our family now, Tiff, and there's no doubting that. I'd 'ave picked you out of a crowd of a million, you look so much like your mum. Come 'ere," he says, and he lifts me up, like I was a five-year-old again and hugs me tight. I hug him back and bury my face in his warm neck. Then my grandma joins in too, and I know for sure that I'm in the right place. That I'm home at last.

When I'm all tucked up in bed, I pick up the photo of my mum and me and kiss her face and stroke her ice-blonde hair. I try to imagine what Christmas in prison must be like. I wonder if she'll have a proper Christmas dinner and if they even have a tree. When will she be allowed to open the cards and presents that we sent to her? I wonder if she's lonely, thinking of us all here together. My anger melts into a heavy kind of sad puddle that's lying in my chest. I feel guilty. I'm beginning to like it here. I'm beginning to like having a new life and a new family and although I do miss my mum, I don't miss how our life was. I don't miss everything being so unpredictable all the time. I don't miss her going out at night and leaving me alone. And I don't miss worrying about her wandering fingers and being embarrassed about her stealing.

I draw a little heart on the picture glass and give it wings to make it fly. I blow my hand and watch it zoom through the window, out into the Sarkian stars. I watch it whizzing across the cold, dark sea and all the way to London, to my mum in her grey prison cell. I imagine her catching it and tucking it under her covers and hugging it tight. I tuck our photo under my covers and cuddle it tight too, and it almost feels like we're together again.

Chapter 24

It's Chriiiiiiiiiiiiistmaaaaaaaaasssssss . . .

Indigo comes charging into my room at the crack of dawn.

"Gwake up, Tiff," she squeals. "It's Chriiiiiiiiiiiiiistmaaaaaaaaaasssssss!"

"OK, OK," I say, pulling a hoodie on over my pyjamas. "Let's go see what Santa left for us, shall we?"

We race downstairs into the sitting room. It's piled high with presents for everyone, glittering under the tree. I switch on the fairy lights and unhook two fat stockings that are swinging from the mantelpiece. Indigo and I scoff the chocolates from our stockings and watch Christmas TV while we wait for everyone else to wake up.

"I glove you, Tiff," she says in her thumb-speak, snuggling up on my lap.

"I love you too," I say, feeding her another mini chocolate Santa. "And I'm sorry if I've been a bit mean."

After our proper breakfast, when everyone's showered and dressed, Grandpa clinks a spoon against a glass, calling for everyone's attention.

"Now family," he laughs, "before we get down to some serious present opening, I think we all need a little breath of fresh air. What do you think Cass, Dan, Margie?"

Uncle Dan winks, "Good idea." He smiles.

"Gno!" shrieks Indigo. "Presents! Presents!"

I don't really want fresh air, either, but this style of Christmas is new to me, so I stand on the edge and smile. Grandpa leads the way, and we all head out through the garden towards the derelict barn. It's a cold, crisp day and I'd rather be inside, toasting by the fire. The sky is bright blue and the sun is smiling down. A quiet hush has wrapped itself around our little island

and only the church bells break its spell. We trudge past the barn and go through the gate that leads on to one of our fields. In the distance I can see silver tinsel dancing on the breeze and shining in the sun. Then I notice what the tinsel is attached to, and Indigo does too. I gasp and hold my breath, not quite believing, and Indigo squeals and leaps into Grandpa's arms.

A tiny brown pony is bobbing its way towards us and a bigger dapple-grey pony is trotting along beside.

"Look what Father Christmas left for my two little princesses, then," says Grandpa, finding magic apples behind our ears.

For a moment, I can't actually quite believe that the dapple-grey pony standing in front of me is actually mine. I have to keep blinking and pinching myself to make sure it's true. And a part of me is scared in case someone takes her away.

Grandpa puts his arm round my shoulder. "She really *is* yours Tiff, I promise, and no one's going to take her away."

I hold out my hand to make friends with my pony. Her muzzle is soft and her gentle eyes are warm and calm. I move closer and she snorts, tickling pony breath into my ears and muzzling close, inviting me to stroke her. I gently hug her, giving her time to get used to me, and rest my cold cheek on her warm neck, breathing her in. I thread my fingers through her creamy mane, plaiting us together, making us friends, forever. Now I'm completely excited and fizzing all over and tears are welling up in my eyes. I'm so surprised I can hardly breathe, but somehow the words "Thank you" escape from my lips and dance on the breeze. I never, ever dreamed I'd ever have a pony of my own and here she is, all mine.

In a flash I realise that I'm not a London girl any more, who lives in a flat and shops all the time and goes out for slap-up meals. I'm a country girl who likes outside and stars and who really is friends with a weird tree-house boy and a kind girl who likes to keep everyone happy but herself.

After we've patted and stroked our ponies some more and fed them their Christmas apples, we tear ourselves away and go back to the house. I text Max and Isla to tell them my exciting news and to say sorry for being such a rubbish friend. When we've opened all our other presents and eaten our humongus lunch and played silly party games and checked on our ponies at least seven hundred times, I slip away to my room.

I have a very important letter to write.

Dear Mum,

Happy Christmas. I love you, but I've been angry with you lately. I was scared with everything changing so fast. I feel a bit better now, although I still don't understand why you did what you did.

Grandpa and Grandma are amazing, they remind me of you, all blond and bling and loud and funny. Santa brought me a pony and one for Indigo too. Mine's a dapple-grey cob called Stardust and Indigo's is a tiny Shetland pony called Cupcake. Auntie Cass is going to teach me to ride, and for Christmas she bought me a riding hat and all the stuff I need. She is lovely, and even though I haven't been very kind to her, she's looking after me really well.

There's this old barn here that Uncle Dan keeps going on about wanting to do up. It is gross and mouldy at the moment, but he wants to turn it into a shiny new home for us, for when you come out of prison. And I haven't wanted it until today, but I've got Stardust now and the barn looks out over the field where she lives, so I would be able to keep a good eye on her. Pleeeaasssseeeee can we stay here?

I hope you like the recording of my school concert that we sent you and the portrait of me. My friend Max drew it and I hope you're not angry that I cut my hair. I had to do it, I'm sorry, but I'm growing it long again now. And I hope that your Christmas is fun and that you're not too sad.

Come home soon, Mum, please.

You and me, Mum. You and me xxxxxxxxxxxx

Chapter 25

Making you Shine...

It's January and my grandpa and grandma have gone back to Spain and have promised we can all go and visit them in the summer holidays, hopefully with my mum, if she's back home by then. Uncle Dan is busy drawing the plans for the barn and employing some builders to do the work. On the plans he's drawn in a bedroom for me that actually overlooks the pony field, so I can watch Stardust and Cupcake from my bedroom window and make sure they're OK. That's if we can persuade my mum to come and live here. I'm keeping my fingers crossed.

Max says I've become pony obsessed and is worried that I might turn out like his mum. Well, he's right, a bit, because I've covered my white bedroom walls with pony posters and with some sketches that I've done myself. Max bought me a sketchbook and some proper artists' pencils for Christmas and he's teaching me how to draw. I'm nowhere near as good as him, but at least I'm not as rubbish as I'd thought I was. And when I'm not reading about ponies, or drawing them, I'm off trekking round the island with Isla and Max or grooming them or picking up poo. And I've started a Friday-night film club at the school, and we're busily working our way through all my old movies. On our first night we watched *The Wizard of Oz*, which made me miss Chelsea millions. I wish she was here too, joining in all my fun, still being my bestie. Isla's slowly getting the hang of doing American accents and remembering all the words, but she'll never be as good as Chels. Max doesn't love old films as much as me and he doesn't love ponies, but he comes along anyway and is teaching me loads about how to ride.

At the weekends we watch films, go for rides, drink hot chocolate at Kristina's café, and then all huddle in Max's tree house, drawing or playing games. Chelsea wouldn't recognise me any more, nor would my mum because I'm mostly muddy and windswept and my hair's a mess. Sometimes I don't even recognise myself. One day, Auntie Cass takes a photo of me and Indigo on our ponies. We put it in a shiny silver frame and send it to Mum. A few days later I have a letter back.

Hi Tiff,

Thanks for your Christmas letter, babe. I miss you and love you so much and I'm so, so sorry for messing up. If I could change things I would, but I can't. All I can do is apologise and promise never to get us into such a mess again. I'm sorry for leaving you at nights and for drinking so much I couldn't stand up. I'm sorry for stealing stuff that I thought would make you happy and not noticing that you were scared. It's only now that I haven't got you around every day that I realise that none of that was important. The only important thing was me loving you and you loving me. And I know I haven't done a very good job of that so far. But I plan to make it up to you, Tiff, I promise.

Auntie Cass will explain things to you in a bit more detail, but basically, my case has been to court and because you don't have another parent to care for you, and because I've been a very good girl while I've been here, I should be out of here at the beginning of March. The judge said that really I should stay here for a whole year, but having you got me off, Tiff. I'm lucky. Mikey's been put away for years, so that's the end of him and good riddance I say!

I'm not sure about coming back to Sark. So much has happened there in the past, Tiff, that it scares me. I don't know how to unravel it all and start again. I don't even know if I'd be welcome. I upset a lot of people who were very special to me and I don't know if they'll ever be able to forgive me. But we'll see. Let's give it time.

Mostly, I'm sorry for running away from my family and for never letting you have the chance to know them. But I'm glad you do now and I'm glad they're enjoying you and you're enjoying them. I've been a silly girl in my life, Tiff, and I'm paying the price and learning my lesson the hard way. Don't let that happen to you.

You look wonderful on Stardust and your hair looks great, I hardly recognise you, you've changed so *much. It's like happiness is just streaming out of you, making you shine. I'm so proud of you, take care my beautiful girl; I hope that one day you'll be able to forgive me.*

All my bestest and biggest and fattest and truest love,

Mama xxxx

P.S. You won't believe it, Tiff, but my cooking's getting more brilliant by the day! My tutor says I'm a natural and that I should think about going into business. xx

I open up the back of the photo frame that holds the picture of my mum and me and tuck her letter inside to keep it safe. Then I close it up, stroke her hair and kiss her photo face. I put the frame back beside my bed facing out, so that she can look at me when I'm sleeping. It's good to hear from her, but I suddenly feel nervous and jumpy inside. My mum sounds different. It feels like prison has made her stop pretending. And hearing her admit to leaving me alone at night and drinking too much and actually noticing I was scared makes a hard stone grow in my throat, which I can't swallow down.

She's never said stuff like that to me before. She's only ever laughed it off and covered it up, and I've always gone along, pretending and icing up the cracks, making it better all the time. But now she's telling the truth, I feel like I'm falling into a black hole, losing my footing, losing what's familiar.

A little panic bubble rises up inside me. If she's leaving prison at the beginning of March that means there's only about five weeks left to go. Of course I do want to see her, and I do want her to come home, I miss her, I love her, she's my mum. But a scared part of me still wants to rub her out, wants to be Auntie Cass and Uncle Dan's girl with Stardust and Indigo and a simple life. I want her back, but I don't want things the same as they were. I love her, but it's easy loving her from here where she can't get into trouble and she can't mess up.

What's it going to be like when she's back? What's *she* going to be like? And will I ever actually be able to forgive her and trust her again? It all feels too much, too soon. Of course, I want to forgive her but Matilda is right. Every time I dig down deep, the hurt is still just sitting there, waiting to jump out at me, waiting to scratch my face and stab my heart.

Chapter 26

I hope so, sweetheart. . .

Work on the barn is happening fast. Every day the builders swarm on it and buzz away with their tools, bashing and hammering and fixing and building.

"How are we going to persuade my mum that she *has* to come and live here?" I ask Auntie Cass, when we're putting the finishing touches to a batch of cupcakes we've made for tonight's school disco. Indigo's face and hands are covered in pink icing and she's busy scooping leftovers from the bowl.

"I'm not sure," she says, "but knowing your mum we have to do it in a way that makes her feel like it was her idea all along. Carla hates being told what to do by anyone."

"You're telling me," I laugh. "She gets like a toddler in a tantrum if she doesn't have things her own way. Whenever I come up with an idea for anything, she always turns it into her own personal brilliant invention. But in her letters it sounds like this whole prison thing has shocked her and changed her, Auntie Cass. D'you think that's really possible?"

"I hope so, sweetheart," she says, dobbing a blob of pink icing on the end of my nose. "For all our sakes. And in some ways she doesn't have a lot of options. Your old flat's been cleared and the landlord's rented it out to someone else, so you can't go back there. And truthfully, it wouldn't be good for her to move back to the same area, you know with all the gossip and stuff and mixing with the same bad lot."

Then a thought hits me like lightning.

"I've got it!" I say, arranging the cakes on a plate. "It's perfect!"

"Well, go on," says Auntie Cass, "fill us in, share your inspiration."

"Well," I say, "in my mum's last letter she says she's become brilliant at cooking. And, I was just thinking, that well. . ."

"Come on, Tiff, spit it out, the suspense is killing me, you've got a great idea fizzing away in that brain of yours!"

"Well," I say, "I was just thinking, that soon it's going to be summer and, well, the hotel's going to get busy and you're going to need a cook, because you and Uncle Dan won't be able to do everything on your own, and I was just thinking that maybe my mum could do the cooking? She's learned how to in prison and she says she's really good at it."

"You clever, clever girl," says Auntie Cass, mopping Indigo's face with a damp cloth. "The only question is, how do we get your mum to think it's her own idea?"

"Leave it to me," I wink. I pour myself some juice, pick up a spare cupcake that's just asking to be eaten and run upstairs to my room. I settle at my desk and take out some special writing paper with ponies leaping around the edge. Then I start. . .

Dear Mum,

Thanks for your letter. I've been cooking too. Auntie Cass, Indigo and I have just finished making some cupcakes for our school disco tonight and they're

delicious. I'm eating one now, looking out of my bedroom window.

Auntie Cass and Uncle Dan are a bit stressy today. The hotel's getting busy and they're worried about how they're going to manage all the cooking through the summer, when all the tourists arrive. Their old chef just left and they're having trouble finding someone who's a brilliant cook. Mandy has applied for the job and Auntie Cass is thinking about giving her a trial run, but there's some stuff she says she's just not that good at, so she's not really sure.

It's not our problem though, is it? We've got enough of our own problems to deal with in deciding what's going to happen when you leave prison. I mean, I know I wrote to you the other day saying that you and Mandy could work things out, but now I'm not so sure it's a good idea. I've been thinking that it actually might be more fun if we moved back to London. You're right, it's a bit quiet and boring here. Nothing ever happens here at school except work, work and more work. There are no fights to watch to spice up my day. And maybe you could even get a job, as a school cook, that would be fun, Mum, wouldn't it?

And I agree, why would you want to come back here to people who used to love you a lot? With everything that's gone on they might have changed their minds. It's just not worth the risk.

Anyway, I love you millions, although I am a bit nervous about seeing you again. Are you nervous about seeing me?

Love Tiff. You and me, Mum. You and me xxxxxxxxx

P.S. I know you don't like talking about old stuff, but I've been thinking about loads of stuff and I'm curious to know what my dad's name is.

P.P.S. What's going to happen? Do I come to prison and meet you when you get out and then we catch the bus to our new home, or what?

I show Auntie Cass and Uncle Dan my letter.

"You're brilliant, Tiff," says Auntie Cass. "If she's anything like the sister I remember, she'll fall for it big time. Let's post it quick and keep our fingers crossed."

Chapter 27

I've never seen anything so amazing...

"I don't believe it," groans Isla, climbing up the tree-house ladder with a large letter in her hand. "I got in. I passed the stupid school entrance exam. I tried really hard to mess it up, but I still got in. Now what am I going to do?"

"Just tell them, Isla," says Max, filling jars with fresh leaves for his insects to eat. "Just tell them the truth and be done with it."

"Go on," I say. "You can do it Isla; there's no point in keeping on pretending. You'll just get in deeper and deeper until one day you'll find yourself being shipped off to a school you don't want to go to."

Isla buries her head in her hands and starts crying.

"It's just the worst news ever. My mum's ecstatic, she's practically ordering my uniform already and I'm not even due to start until September. I think today is the worst day of my whole life."

"Maxie baby," calls a voice from the bottom of the ladder, "come here a minute."

Isla and I snigger. "Maxie baby" groans and pokes his head through the trap door.

"Hi, Mum," says Max.

"I think Midnight's about to foal, and I thought you and the girls might like to come down to the field and watch? You'll have to be ultra quiet and still," she says, "but I thought you might enjoy the experience."

Max looks at us and shrugs, "D'you fancy it?"

"Do we? Of course we do, Max!" I squeal.

Max gathers up some pencils and a sketchbook and we head off towards the field. It's Valentine's Day and me and Isla are busy mulling over possible foal names. I like Romeo and Cupid best, and Isla likes Valentine and Sweetheart. Max sticks his fingers down his throat and pretends to make himself sick.

"Girls are so dumb," he laughs.

When we get to the field we all huddle in a heap, close

to the hedge. Midnight is walking round and round in circles, panting and swishing and looking all agitated. Her ears are twitching back and she keeps twisting around, staring at her tummy. Max's Mum offers some sweets around, and I don't even bother to look at what I'm eating, I can't take my eyes off Midnight.

Suddenly a big white bag thing pops out of Midnight and water gushes everywhere. She lies down and her panting gets louder. I'm holding my breath, waiting and waiting to see what happens next. Isla is smiling so much I think her face might split in two, and as usual, Max is busy drawing the whole event. He's done little sketches of Midnight and of his mum and loads of Isla and me. And all around the edge of the page he's drawn these amazing rosebuds and cartoon hearts. Suddenly, a little hoof appears and then another and then I see a soft, wet foal nose and a face with big eyes. Max's mum is whispering to us all the time, telling us what's happening.

"The white stuff is the placental sac," she says. "The foal's been growing inside it, swimming in the fluid, for almost a whole year now."

I've never seen anything so amazing in my whole,

entire life. Ever. Midnight is panting and pushing and the rest of the little foal's body shoots out fast and flops on the floor. The placental sac is still covering its body and sits like a wet hoodie over its sweet black head. As it falls away the foal peers around, breathing in its first gasp of air, seeing the world for the very first time. Midnight lies back, puffing and snorting. She rolls over and pulls herself up. Then she's nuzzling her baby and licking its face. Max's mum hops up and pulls the sac away from the foal and checks that everything's OK.

"It's a filly," she says, "a sweet little girl." She gives Midnight a big hug and whispers into her ear. "Well done, girl, well done."

After a while, the filly tries to stand up. At first she's funny, all legs and knees, and wobbly, then she finds strength in her back legs and pushes herself up. Her front legs follow, trying to steady her, stopping her from toppling over. Suddenly, she sort of reminds me of myself, finding my way into my own new life.

Later, when we're back in the tree house, Max shows us his sketches.

"You were, like, non-stop drawing, Max," I say. "Did you actually see the birth?"

"Course I did, dummy," he laughs. "It's just that I see the world through pictures, you know, things make more sense to me when I draw them."

"Chelsea was amazing at drawing as well. You really should get yourself tested for dyslexia, Max," I tease. "You might even find that you do have a brain after all! A bit like the Tin Man in *The Wizard of Oz*."

"What is it with that film, Tiff? You're totally obsessed."

"Oh, I don't know," I say, "I guess I like the idea that everything we need is usually right under our noses. You know, Dorothy travelled all the way along the yellow brick road to ask the Wizard how to find her way home, only to be told that she just had to click her ruby slippers and believe she was there already. I think we should all start believing in ourselves more often."

"A bit like me," sighs Isla, "finding the courage to talk to my parents."

Max rolls his eyes. "Please, don't go all philosophical on me."

169

Just then Max's mum pops her head through the trap door. "Wasn't it amazing? The foal's doing well but it looks like Midnight's in a spot of trouble. The vet's on her way, so can you get yourself some supper Max? I'll be busy for a while."

"I'm sure I'll manage," sighs Max. And I know he's wishing he were the foal or Midnight so his mum would spare some time for him. "What are we gonna call her, Mum?" he says.

"Mmmmm, not sure, does anyone have any ideas?"

"Well," I say, "as it's Valentine's Day, I was thinking of Cupid or Romeo, but neither would really work for a girl."

"I like Sweetheart or Valentina" says Isla.

"What about you, Max, any ideas?"

Max smiles and taps his sketchbook with his pencil.

"You see, if you thought in pictures like me, you'd have seen that her name was right under your nose all along. Look at the white blaze on her forehead, it's exactly the same shape as a rosebud."

Then he tears two pages of sketches out of his book and gives one to Isla and one to me. Mine has loads of tiny sketches of Midnight and the foal to add to my wall, and Isla's has loads of drawings of her surrounded by rosebuds and the cartoon hearts.

"Her name's Rosebud," he says. And we all agree.

Chapter 28

I eat my cake in little nibbles...

Indigo and I always race home from school, and guess what? She always wins. Except today is different. We've had these freak snowstorms and the whole island is knee-deep in snow. It's all right for tractors because they can plough through it without any trouble, but for us it means we have to slip and slide and crunch our way home. Max is busy making massive snowballs and keeps trying to drop them down the back of my coat. I get my own back by sending a big one flying through the air that lands on his head. His red cheeks are dripping with tiny bits of ice, and snowflakes flutter and dance on his eyelashes and hair.

"Got you," I squeal.

He slides towards me with a handful of frosty flakes that's heading for my face.

"And I got you back," he cheers, covering me in snow.

"Glet's make snow gangels," says Indigo. And we all collapse on the floor laughing and giggling and making angel wings in the snow with our arms.

When Indigo and I get home, Uncle Dan is waiting for us with steaming mugs of hot chocolate, thick slices of honey cake, a roaring fire and a white envelope for me.

My heart leaps about in my chest. I know it's from my mum because of the stamp on the front that says HMP Henmoore. And I know that the rest of my life will be changed by the words she's written inside. If she says we have to go back to London it means that I'll have to leave my new family and my friends and, worst of all, Stardust behind, and that doesn't even feel possible right now. I suppose at least I'd have Chelsea and my old school back, but London life actually seems boring compared to here. But if my mum says we can stay here on Sark, forever. . . Well, I'll burst with excitement and squeal for joy.

I eat my cake in little nibbles to make it last longer and sip my drink in long, slow sips. The letter keeps winking at me, waiting to be opened, waiting for me to discover what my future will be.

"Go on," encourages Uncle Dan. "You won't know until you open it," he says.

"I'm scared," I say. "What will I do if she says we can't stay?"

"Well, you won't know until you open it, will you? You might not even have to worry about it. Go on."

So I pick up the envelope and slowly open it.

Hi, babe,

I hope you and Indigo are enjoying all the snow. I've seen it on telly and it looks amazing. Remember to wrap up warm so you don't catch any nasty chills.

I'm having second thoughts about London, Tiff. I know you say you're missing it and I'm sure you must be missing Chelsea loads, but I'm not so sure that moving back is such a good idea. I hope you won't be too disappointed.

I have had this brilliant idea, though, I hope you like it. Anyway, here goes. I get released from here on March 6th, only twelve days to go. Yay! And I was thinking that I could come straight over and start working in the hotel kitchen. You know, we could try it out, no promises to stay forever, but it would be a good place to start. I've told my cookery teacher my brilliant plan and she's got me going on all the special sauces and types of hotel food, so I'll be well prepared when I arrive. Show this letter to Auntie Cass and Uncle Dan and write back soon to let me know what you all think. I'm so excited; I hope you all say yes! And tell them to say no to Mandy, she's not a good idea.

And you're right, Tiff, I did hurt a lot of people, but they loved me once and I hope they'll be prepared to give me a second chance. I'll have to work hard to earn their respect, but this prison experience has changed me, Tiff, for the better. You'll see when I get home. I'm so nervous and excited all at once, I can't stop dancing about. The girls all think I've gone crazy – nothing new there then!

I love you millions and millions and more and more.

You and me, babe. You and me.

Love Mama xxx

P.S. There's nothing much to know about your dad, Tiff, except that he was the love of my life. He did a runner before you were born, and I haven't heard from him since.

P.P.S. His name's Billy.

The smile that's spreading its way across my face and lighting me up like a lighthouse tells Uncle Dan everything he needs to know.

"Brilliant news, Tiff?" he asks.

"Brilliant news!" I smile.

Auntie Cass comes in from the snow, throws off her boots at the door and tumbles into the sitting room.

"So?" she asks. "What did she say? Please tell me she said yes."

"She said yes," I smile. "She said yes and she'll actually be home in twelve days."

Auntie Cass is almost more excited than me. She dances Indigo around the room, gives Uncle Dan a big wet kiss on the lips and hugs me tight.

"I never want to lose you, Tiff, I'm the happiest woman alive."

And I'm the happiest girl alive. Except for one thing: Holly. She's still hassling me now that we're back at school, making comments and blackmailing me to do her homework. But I don't even care about her right now. I run out to Stardust to tell her my good news and run up to my bedroom to write a speedy reply to Mum. This letter is easy. I draw a big pink heart on the page and in the middle write "YES" using my special silver pen. I stuff the letter in an envelope, quickly finish off Holly's homework, then swish my icy way to the post box. I still feel weird addressing a letter to my mum in prison, but hopefully this will be the last time. Sometimes, in the pit of my stomach, I still feel like it's me that's done something wrong, like it's me who should be feeling guilty.

I slide over to Max's tree house wishing I could spill my news, wishing I could tell him that my brilliant plan to get my mum to live here has worked. But I can't because nobody knows about what's happening with my mum, except Holly of course. I squish my happy, excited sparkles into my heart and I wonder if you can see them glowing from the outside.

"Hi Max," I say, peeping my head through the trap door. "Anyone at home?"

"I'm here," he says, "and so's Isla."

I climb up into the tree house. Isla's face turns bright red and Max jumps up and starts busying himself with his insect collection. I suddenly feel a bit awkward but I don't know why.

"I'm not interrupting anything, am I?" I say.

"Er, no," says Isla, looking more like a tomato every minute. "I just popped over 'cause I left my jumper here at the weekend."

Everyone goes quiet. Max starts cleaning out his stick insects and Isla starts gazing at him, like she's suddenly superly interested in what he's doing. Her eyes go all misty and dreamy and take on that faraway look that my mum gets when she's watching a romantic film. My mind suddenly makes the connection. Max and Isla! Never! This is too weird for words.

"I had a letter from my mum today," I say to break the spell. "She's finishing her job and coming over to Sark in twelve days time. She says we can stay here, on the island. I won't have to go back to London, ever. I'm so excited."

And the three of us jump up and down and dance around like crazy people until Max's mum comes to tell us to be quiet, because she can hear us from the field.

Chapter 29

D.O.N.T...

My mum arrives on Sark in three days' time and I'm actually really starting to panic. I've kind of got used to not having her around and used to asking Auntie Cass and Uncle Dan if I need help with anything, or if I can go out with my friends and stuff like that. And I'm worried that when my mum gets back everything's just going to feel all confusing again. When my mum knows that I have a routine and I go up to bed at nine and read for half an hour, she's just going to burst out laughing at me. She'll think it's a ridiculous thing to do because she'll want me to stay up late and keep her company and have fun watching movies and eating snacks. Then I'm going to be stuck not knowing what to do, or who to please. And I really hope that she's not going to be embarrassing all the time and all loud and attention-seeking, like she was in London. I feel really guilty feeling like this, but I like my new life and although I miss her and want her to come home, in some ways it would be much easier if she could just stay where she is and not interfere.

For some reason we all decide it's a good idea to have a grand clean up before Mum comes home. Everyone's a bit nervous and edgy and we find that keeping busy helps to calm us all down. We start on the downstairs and move our way up like a big cleaning machine, dusting, Hoovering, washing and straightening. Uncle Dan finds a spare mattress in the hotel storeroom and we put it in my room for Mum. The barn's not quite finished, so she'll have to share with me for a few weeks, until it's ready for us to move in.

Me and Indigo head out into the field and we give Stardust and Cupcake their very own pony makeovers. We brush them until they're gleaming and smooth, make loads of little plaits all along their manes, and brush their forelocks straight and long. We pick up all the poo in sight and make sure there's no rubbish in the field.

When we're finished I go inside, run up to the bathroom and lock myself in. I stare in the mirror and a worried-looking girl stares right back at me. It's easy to make the house and the ponies and the field look smart and clean, but what about me? What will my mum think of me being all covered in mud all the time, with grubby nails and scruffy hair? *Look at you*, says my reflection in the mirror, *you're a state. Your hair's grown all wonky and your face always seems to have either mud or cake crumbs all over it. And your clothes, just look at them; you look like you've been dragged through a hedge backwards. What will your mum say? You're a mess Tiffany Morris and there's no getting away from it.*

"Shut up," I shout at my reflection, "shut up, shut up, shut up, it doesn't matter, none of that stuff matters any more. I'm tired of keeping her happy all the time. I need to keep myself happy too and say what I want for my life sometimes, like Isla needs to. And anyway, I like being like this. I like being muddy and cakey and tangly. And I don't even care what you say."

Do.

"Don't."

Do, do, do.

"I don't," I shout. "Do you get it? D. O. N. T. spells DON'T! And if she gets in a mood then it's her problem, not mine."

Chapter 30

Toffee slipped on the ice...

Only two days to go, it's Saturday, and I need some fresh air and some time alone. I tell Auntie Cass I'm going for a walk and head off towards the woods. The snow is still thick in places, and bright sunshine sparkles through the winter trees. Brave little snowdrops peep their hats above the soil, and snowy silence drifts on the wind. School is fine, except for Holly who still hangs over me like a bad smell. She knows my mum's coming home soon and is threatening to leak our secret to the whole island. I told her she was taking things too far. But she's not letting up. "A deal is a deal, Tiffany Morris," she'd said, pushing me against the wall.

Max has gone off somewhere with his mum and wouldn't say where. And poor Isla has gone to an open day at her expensive boarding school. Obviously, she didn't tell her parents that she really doesn't want to go and somehow I don't think she ever will. I've promised to take Indigo to a jumble sale in the Island Hall at two o'clock. Indigo and me love rummaging through all the old stuff and cycling home with our bike baskets full. It's even more fun than shopping in actual shops because there are so many treasures waiting to be discovered. But right now I just need some thinking time alone.

Since living on Sark I've discovered that walking is a good way of getting rid of my life worries. Every step usually makes them float away on the breeze, far, far out to sea where they belong, helping to clear my mind. But today it's not working because my worries are big. Very big. I'm really panicking now about how things are going to be when my mum comes home. It's a weird feeling. Like I'm meeting my mum for the first time, or something. Then I go off on some daydream about what it would be like to meet my dad for the first time.

My snowy silence is broken by a loud snapping twig,

which makes me jump. Then a heavy thud noise travels on the air. I hear a pony neighing somewhere ahead of me and a girl screaming and I freeze, not knowing what to do.

"Help," calls the girl's voice. "Please somebody, help me."

I charge forward in the direction of the girl's voice. She sounds frightened and keeps on calling and calling.

"Hang on," I shout. "I'm coming."

I come to a clearing in the trees, and there on the wet, snowy ground is Holly, clutching her ankle and whimpering with pain. She has a massive bump on her forehead and a bleeding cut on the side of her face.

"Oh," I say, backing off, "it's you."

"Toffee slipped on the ice and I fell off. I think he's really badly hurt his knee and my ankle's killing me. I don't think I can manage to get up."

"Holly, what are you doing out here on your own in the ice? Where's your mum?" I'm frozen to the spot and I don't know what to do.

"I had a really bad argument with her and needed some time to think. I was stupid to come out in this

186

weather and now it's all my fault that Toffee's hurt," she cries. "Please, I need your help, Tiff."

"Well, you're right, you are stupid to ride alone in this weather, and why should I bother with you anyway? You've been so mean to me, Holly, and if I had any sense I'd walk away right now and leave you to freeze." I grab Toffee's reigns and try to calm the pony down.

"Please don't leave me, Tiff," she cries, "I might die out here if you go."

"And if I help, then what happens, you get better and then carry on bullying me like nothing's changed?"

"No," she whimpers, feeling the blood on her face. "I'll stop. I'll leave you alone, anything you say, just don't leave me, Tiff, please. I need to get home."

"Of course I'll help but you have to tell me why you and your mum hate me and my mum so much."

"I promise," she cries, wincing with pain.

"And you need to stop trying to own Isla, she's her own person you know, with feelings, she's not a toy."

She nods. I move closer to her.

"OK, Holly," I sigh. "I'm here. Do you think you can stand?"

"I'll have a go," she says, taking my arm. I pull her

up and put her arm around my shoulder, taking her weight. Toffee's looking nervous and he's walking with a limp.

"Right, hold on tightly to me and let's give it a go."

And together we slowly hobble and slide back through the woods, out towards Holly's house. Toffee's taking his time and Holly's really worried that his injury is bad. She can feel her ankle swelling up inside her boot, so we try taking it off to have a look, but it hurts her too much so we keep on going.

"D'you think it's broken?" I ask.

"I don't think so," she says. "I'm more worried about poor old Toffee, it'll be terrible if he's hurt his knee. If he goes lame my mum might even force me to have him put down."

I rub her shoulder to make her feel better, then I remember that she was going to tell me what happened to make our mum's hate each other. "I want to know everything," I say. "All the details."

"Well, I don't really know much myself," she says, "but I think it all started years ago when our mums were best friends. Your mum kept stealing things from mine. And it was OK when it was small stuff, but it just got bigger and bigger until your mum ran off with my mum's boyfriend. And then a few months later I came along and it's just been me and her ever since. That's why she's so mad. Your mum stole the love of her life and he was my dad too. So I've never even seen him. And I don't even now his name. I keep asking my mum but she never says."

"Well, you're not the only one, you know. That's exactly what my mum says about my dad too. He ran off just before I was born and I've never seen him either. It's always been just Mum and me. That's why I had to come here when she went away."

Now I can understand why Mandy is so angry. "I'm sorry, Holly. My mum does get herself in a mess sometimes. But she's changed, you know."

"I'm sorry too," says Holly.

I can't believe Holly is apologising to me!

"I didn't want to be mean to you," she's saying. "I just followed my mum instead of thinking for myself. We always look out for each other. And I'm sorry about your mum and prison and everything. It must have been really scary."

"Yeah, it was," I say. "Well, it looks like we've got

more in common than we thought, Holly Hutchinson. Come on." And then we start laughing, but that makes Holly's foot hurt even more so we smother our giggles and hobble on home.

Chapter 31

Holly's mouth drops open...

"What's your mum like?" asks Max. It's after school the next day and we're up in the tree house playing a board game. Even Holly's there with her sprained ankle in a white bandage.

"Well, she's kind of a bit mad," I laugh. "In a crazy, silly, fun way."

My mind runs a mini-film of Mum on one of her crazy days. "And, she's got a bit of a temper," I say, thinking of good ways to describe her. "Oh and she likes wearing a *lot* of perfume and very clean white clothes and boots and loads of jewellery. And she has ice-blonde hair and goes to the tanning salon every week, so she

 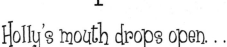

has a great suntan even when it's snowing. But she is nice, *really*."

Holly's mouth drops open. "That's exactly what my mum said she'd be like by now. She overheard someone saying your mum was coming back to live here and she's not very pleased. I told her that it's good to give people a second chance because we all mess up sometimes."

"And what did she say to that?" asks Max.

"She said there'll be no second chances, not ever. She says that Tiff's mum made her bed when she messed up years ago and she'd have to learn to lie on it now."

"Oooh, harsh," says Max. "I don't wanna be around when they first meet up."

"I do," says Isla. "It'll be the most dramatic thing that's happened on Sark for a hundred years or more. Except for Holly and Tiff making friends, that is."

Holly and I smile at each other. We're both mega-relieved that Toffee's injury wasn't so bad. And Isla is positively over the moon and back about us being friends, but she's still acting weird around Max.

"D'you wanna borrow my jumper, Isla?" he says. "You look chilly."

Isla turns red. "Er, OK," she smiles. "Thanks."

Holly raises her eyebrows at me and we share a secret chuckle. "Are you two. . . you know. . .?" she asks.

Both their faces start glowing so red I can almost see steam coming out of their ears. Max virtually glues both his eyes to the board and takes his turn.

"Well?" persists Holly. "Are you?"

They both look at each other in that weird way again.

"I'm not sure," says Max, searching Isla's eyes. "Are we?"

"I suppose," she shrugs at Max. "If you want?"

"Um, yes, OK," says Max, and I can see that he can hardly hide his massive grin. Then he takes a half-eaten Mars bar out of his pocket and offers her a bite.

"Anyway," Isla says, taking her turn at the game. "I think it's time to change the subject, don't you?"

"Good idea," I say, wanting things to be normal between us all. "Have you got round to telling your parents that you don't want to go away to school yet?"

"No," says Isla. "It's too late, really. Half of my uniform's arrived already and my mum's gone ahead and accepted the place."

We all look at her. Speaking up and saying what you really want is hard, especially when your mum has big fat ear plugs in her ears so she can't hear what you're saying, anyway.

"How about speaking to your dad?" says Max. "He might listen."

"No," shrugs Isla. "He always just goes along with what my mum says."

Just then my mobile pings into life, and there's a message from Auntie Cass asking me to go home.

"Got to go," I say, leaping up and wrapping the scarf Isla gave me for Christmas round my neck. "Let Woody the stick insect take my place in the game. You'll be OK, Isla. See you soon, cheesy moons."

"In a while, salami smile," they all chant back.

Chapter 32

Frozen to the spot...

On my way home I practise riding my bike with no hands. Max's been trying to teach me for ages, but I can still only manage a few pedal turns without starting to wobble, especially when it's dark and I've only got my bike light to guide me home. I feel a bit weird, about him and Isla liking each other. It's not that I'm jealous in *that* kind of way, because I definitely don't *fancy* boys or anything, it's just that it changes things and I'm still getting used to how it feels when everything flips.

A cold wind is hurling itself around the island and the dark sky is full of spring drizzle. I dump my bike in the shed and go indoors. I'm glad to be home.

"Hi everyone," I call, throwing off my coat and shoes and untangling my scarf from my neck, "I'm back."

No one answers and a spooky silence wafts its way into the hall, "Heelloooo, anybody hooomme?" I say in a silly ghost voice.

More silence. I guess everyone's busy in the hotel so I decide to get a drink and a biscuit before I go off and find them. It's strange Auntie Cass texting me to come home when nobody's here. I wander into the kitchen and freeze. My heart starts pounding in my chest and my knees start to wobble. An ice-blonde ghost from the past is sitting at the kitchen table. She's waiting for me, and she's not supposed to be here, not until tomorrow.

Help! I don't know if I'm ready. She looks different and worried, like she doesn't know what to say or where to start. And I don't know what to say or where to start either, so I just stand like a dummy, frozen to the spot. I want her to go away. I want her to disappear like ghosts do and stop haunting me. *Please!* I'm not ready until tomorrow. I will be ready then. I'll have planned what to say, I'll have brushed my hair and washed my face and—

"Hello, babe?" she smiles. There's worry dancing in

her eyes and so many unspoken words trying to make their way to her lips. We're caught in a slow motion movie, like wading through glue. "Hello, darling." Why is she doing this to me? It's so typical. Why can't she ever stick to her plans? She's not supposed to be here until *tomorrow*. My legs can't move but my brain is telling them they have to. It's sending lightning signals that are telling me I'm supposed to fly into her arms and sob all over her and say that everything's OK and I'm so glad she's back. And that's what I want to do and what I'd like to say. But a massive angry monster that's been hiding in a dark cave for three long months is pushing its way through the nice words and threatening to burst its way into the room. I swallow hard to keep it down. But my angry feelings are my true feelings right now, and I'm tired of locking them away.

Without saying a single word I walk over to the fridge and find some apple juice. I get two glasses from the dresser shelf and the tin of chocolate brownies that Indigo and I made at the weekend. I sit down at the table opposite Mum, pour us both some juice and offer her a brownie. Her hand shakes when she takes one from the tin and my brownie sits like dry dust in my mouth.

"Why did you come today?" I burst out. "You said tomorrow, I'm not ready."

"I'm sorry, Tiff," her voice wobbles. "It's just, I wanted to slip back on to the island without a big song and dance. I didn't want you to have to wait for me at the harbour and meet me in front of everyone. I felt we needed to be on our own for a bit."

OK, so she has a point. It would've been *too* weird meeting her at the harbour and having to pretend that everything was OK between us. And I get that she wouldn't want too much attention drawn to her and that she wouldn't be ready for everyone's questions, not yet.

"Did Auntie Cass know?" I ask, hoping that she hadn't because I couldn't bear a lie from her.

"No," Mum says, "nobody knew. I arrived here a couple of hours or so ago. I guessed you'd be out with your friends and I needed to talk to Cass, to see how you're doing and how she is and to check out that it's really OK for us to stay here. I didn't want to build our hopes up if she felt that things might not really work out."

"Oh," I say, surprised at quite how well she'd thought the whole thing through. Unusual for my mum.

"I wanted to meet you on your own, Tiff. You know, to get used to each other again. I got Cass to text you, then she, Dan and Indigo popped over to the hotel to give us some space."

"Oh," I say again. My angry monster has sloped away, surprised by the sense that my mum is making. She's sounding like a grown-up and I've never heard her speak like this before. She usually blasts her way into situations and blabbers on without thinking. This is different; she's somehow more real.

"D'you fancy introducing me to Stardust then?"

My eyes light up. "OK."

In the hallway Mum rummages through the shoe pile and pulls on a pair of Auntie Cass's boots that are covered in mud. She leans over, scoops up her hair, and fixes it in a scraggy bun thing with an old pencil from the shelf. Then she eases herself into a tatty green anorak that's hanging on the wall. I pull on my own boots and jacket, grab Uncle Dan's big torch and lead the way out to the field. Mum's warm hand slips its way into mine and gives me a friendly, gentle squeeze. I don't pull away. The wind is blowing even harder now, and an icy drizzle has come out to play with the evening chill. Mum doesn't seem to care one bit about the rain on her hair, or the mud on her boots. And we don't care at all about the salty tears that are creeping out of our eyes, streaming down our faces and stinging our cheeks. Still holding hands, we turn to face each other and I notice, for the first time, that there's no mascara running with my mum's tears and there's no lipstick on her smile. She opens her arms wide and folds me into a warm hug. My body melts into hers, and right then all of the scared and angry monsters that I've been holding on to rise up through my body like hot lava in a volcano. I'm shaking and sobbing and so wet that I can't tell the difference any more between the rain and my tears. My mum just holds me tighter and tighter and we're swaying gently with the wind. She's whispering "I'm sorry, Tiff, I'm sorry," and for the first time ever it's *her* that's making *me* feel better and not the other way around. We stand there for ages and I realise that sometimes a hug is all you need.

"Come on then, Island Girl," she smiles, when all my monsters have been washed away by the rain, "let's see how much you know about ponies, shall we?"

And we start chattering away about riding as if we've

never even been apart for one day. She knows *so* much about horses, stuff that I wouldn't ever have imagined her knowing. And she tells me stuff about living in the countryside that she's always kept to herself, and it feels like I'm meeting my mum for the first time. I have to keep touching her to make sure she's real. And she's going to teach me everything she knows about riding, and she might even get a horse of her own.

In the last three months our whole world has tipped itself upside down and been shaken around so everything's in a different place. And although we've both been hurting and frightened and sad, the love that's always been there is shining out and brimming over. Suddenly and quietly, without a fuss, my mum is back in my life and I'm back in hers.

"You and me, Tiff," she says when we're walking back to the house.

"You and me, Mum," I smile.

Chapter 33

This is our home...

My mum's been back on Sark for over a week now and everything's brilliant. She's completely taken over the hotel kitchen and is up early most mornings, chopping and mixing and making and baking. We're all really impressed with her, and Uncle Dan says she'll get us such a good reputation for fine food, we'll soon be overflowing with guests all year round. And we're not just flattering her, her cooking really *is* delicious.

When she's not in the kitchen, wearing her special chef's clothes, she just pulls on any old jeans and jumper and hardly even bothers to brush her hair. I'm amazed; she wouldn't have been seen dead like this in London.

But I'm glad because it means she's not fussing all the time and she's not always hassling me to change my clothes and paint my nails and brush my hair. And you wouldn't believe *her* nails for one moment. On day one of being here, she got the clippers out and chop, chop, chopped them all right off.

"It's called 'hygiene', Tiff," she said. "I can't risk letting chips and flakes of old nail varnish fall into the soup, can I?"

Auntie Cass looks like someone has stuck the sunshine inside her and left it permanently switched on. She can't stop grinning from ear to ear, she's so happy to have Mum back home. And they're just like kids when they're together, they giggle about things and tease Uncle Dan and cosy up together with cups of tea and share secrets. Uncle Dan's happy and gets along really well with Mum, but he says it's not fair because he's being overrun with too many female hormones floating about the place. So he's working uber hard to finish the barn. Mum's gone crazy with choosing paint colours for our new walls. There's no more pure white for us, we're going for loads of lovely colours because we want to bring the outside inside. So we're having fresh greens like the trees and grass and soft blues like the sky and the sea and warm yellows like the sunshine. And I never knew my mum liked nature so much. Whenever she has spare time she's always off walking in the woods or heading down the cliffs to the beaches below.

Mum *loves* my new school. She says that the bit in my letter about me going back to my old school was what really put her off of going back to London.

"This is where we belong, Tiff," she says. "This is our home."

The Max and Isla thing is still weirding me and Holly out, but we're getting used to it, slowly. Holly says not to worry because it will probably blow over soon. She said it's hardly like they're getting married, is it? And anyway, as far as anyone knows, Isla will be leaving come September, won't she?

Mum still hasn't bumped into Mandy, and she still won't tell me any more than Holly did.

"Leave it in the past, Tiff," she says "where it belongs. I know she's angry but we'll bump into each other when the time's right. She must know I'm back home by now and she hasn't arrived with her guns blazing, so give it time, Tiff. It'll all work out; trust me. And don't worry about keeping my whole prison escapade a secret. I'm happy for the whole story to come out in the open. No more secrets."

But I'm not used to trusting my mum's promises, and it's a new thing for me. At break time Holly tells me that her mum's gone into a silent huff since my mum's arrival, and Holly doesn't know what to do. I feel sorry for Holly; it's hard when you feel like you're the one who has to look after your mum, I remember.

"I still can't tell her about being friends with you, Tiff, she'd go bananas. It's stupid, I wish they could just sort it out between themselves and let us get on with our lives."

I try my mum again after school.

"Holly doesn't know what to do with Mandy," I say, "she's gone into this huff."

"Oh, well, that's her problem, Tiff. There's nothing much I can do about it is there?"

"Yes, but you could go and see her or something."

"Oh, babe, you won't give up will you? That's one trait you inherited from your dad."

"What?" suddenly forgetting about Mandy and

Holly. At last she's mentioned my dad. "Tell me Mum. What else did I inherit from him? I want to know."

"Well," she smiles, stroking my hair, "you got most of your good looks from my side of the family, of course! But you did get your determination from Billy and your beautiful emerald eyes and your sweet little nose."

"So what happened? How come everything went wrong?"

"We were young, Tiff, really young. Just teenagers. We all used to hang out together and have great parties round the harbour and on the beach. Then things started to get serious between us all and Mandy fell in love with a boy – Billy."

"What? My Dad?"

"Yes." She stops talking and looks down at her lap.

"Go on, Mum," I say.

She takes a deep breath. "One night, we were all sitting there, a bit tipsy from too much cider and he came over to me and said, 'Carla Morris I'm madly in love with you. Let's run away to England.'"

"What? You stole Mandy's boyfriend?" I say.

She pauses again and I tell her she has to finish.

"I looked into his eyes and I just couldn't resist him.

I'd always loved him, you see. I was a teenager, Tiff, so I just packed my bag without telling anyone and hopped on a ferry to Guernsey, and another to England and the rest, as they say, is history."

"But then what happened?"

"Well, we found a cool place to live in London and got some jobs and had some fun and then I got pregnant with you, Tiff. But he said he was too young to be a dad. So one day he just packed his bag and went, just like that, to travel the world. I've never heard from him or seen him again. And he doesn't know what he's missed by not staying around for you. You see, Tiff, he left Mandy and then he left me."

Chapter 34

I wondered if you were. . . you know. . .

It's Saturday morning and my mum has disappeared.

"Don't worry," says Auntie Cass, reading my concern. "She's just popped to the shops. She said she had some secret shopping to do. She'll be back soon."

A knife twists in my tummy. Secret shopping sounds like my mum is up to her old tricks again. I hop on my bike and head off to find her. But she's not at the shops; she's not anywhere. So I whizz round to Max's tree house to see if anyone has seen her. But no one's there, either. Everyone in my life has disappeared.

"Where is everyone?" I ask Stardust when I get back

home. But she's only interested to know if I have an apple for her to munch on.

Finally, after a hundred years, my mum returns as if nothing's happened and gets busy in the hotel kitchen making a cake.

"Where have you been, Mum? I was worried about you."

"I just had to pop out," she smiles. "I had some shopping to do. No big deal, Tiff, don't go getting your knickers in a twist. I don't have to ask your permission these days, do I?"

"No," I say, feeling silly, "but, you know, I wondered if you were, you know. . ."

"No, Tiff, I wasn't, you know. . . anything. I've told you, I'm never doing that again. I'm all straight and above-board these days. No dodgy business, I promise, not ever. You really need to start trusting me."

"Really? Promise?"

"Promise."

"Where were you then?"

"Well, if you must know," she smiles, "I was out buying a birthday present for Mandy. You know, a kind of peace offering. Then I dropped it through her letterbox and now I'm making her favourite birthday cake in the hope that she might pop in and we can sort this all out once and for all."

"How do you know it's her birthday?"

"Well, you tell me when Chelsea's birthday is?"

"Seventh of May," I say, "I'll never forget that."

"There you go then, Little Miss Nosy, end of story. You never forget your best friend's birthday, believe me."

I feel a bit silly now, checking up on my mum, but I'm pleased she's made the first move in sorting things out with Mandy, and I can't wait to see Holly and tell her. Auntie Cass comes into the kitchen to help mum prepare lunch. Uncle Dan's busy cleaning the bar and I'm running around with clean glasses, fresh flowers and cups of tea and coffee. Indigo's dressed up as a fairy princess and is flying about the place sprinkling good luck dust all over the floor. And I feel full to the brim with good luck. I know that anytime I come home from anywhere I just have to pop my head round the door and someone will be in. And I can even pick up the phone and call my grandparents in Spain if I just fancy a chat. I know that some people's families get on their nerves, but mine is totally brilliant. Probably because I've waited so long to get one. I'm the luckiest girl alive. I think about Matilda and send her some good luck fairy dust as well and hope she won't have to wait too much longer for someone to take her home.

The restaurant's busy today and it really is all hands on deck. Lunch is flying out from the kitchen and I'm running backwards and forwards like a mad thing, clearing the tables and taking pudding orders. I'm so busy I don't even notice the door open, but suddenly, standing at the bar, are Mandy and Holly. And Mandy's face is fuming.

"Where is she?" she screams, rummaging in her bag. "Where is that coward of a woman? Come out Carla Morris, wherever you are, and face the music."

Mum hurries out of the kitchen, wiping her hands on a tea towel.

"Keep it down, Mand," she hushes. "If you hadn't noticed, there are people here eating lunch. We've got a business to run."

"Do you think I care about that, Carla," screeches Mandy. "You never cared about anyone in your whole life, so why should I? You've spent forever walking over other people and now it's my turn. See this?" she says waving a small pink parcel in the air and throwing it at Mum's feet. "Do you think you can butter me up with a birthday present? Well you're wrong. I don't want your rotten present, so here, have it back."

Mum looks like she's had her face slapped. She picks up the present and puts it on the bar.

"Well, what do you want from me then? How can I make it all up to you, Mand? Don't you see, it's a peace offering, I want you back, I miss you. I love you."

"And you think you can make it up with a present? You really need to get your head looked at if you think you make up for a whole life of treachery by giving people stupid presents. It's just stuff, Carla. Rubbish. It doesn't mean anything."

"Well, it's a start isn't it, you ungrateful cow?"

"You see the trouble with you, Carla, is that you could never see beyond the stuff. You just wanted more and more of it, more and more things. But look where it got you."

All eyes are on Mandy and my mum. Auntie Cass is standing behind the bar with Uncle Dan and Indigo and Holly's frozen to the spot, looking like a statue with her mouth hanging open. All of the diners have given up eating and are watching like they've suddenly found themselves in the middle of a soap opera. It's clear that this screaming match isn't going to end until someone steps in.

"Enough!" I say and my voice is really loud and clear. "Let's sort this whole thing out, shall we?" I look at my mum who's standing there, covered in cake icing, looking totally baffled, and at Mandy who's fumbling with the buckle on her bag, looking lost and alone.

"It's simple," I say to Mum. "If you want Mandy to trust you again, if you want *everyone* else to trust you again, you might need to *explain* yourself, Mum. And you might want to think about saying sorry?"

She whimpers, looking at me with pleading eyes.

Mandy stares at Mum. Waiting.

"OK," Mum sighs, moving closer to Mandy. "Here goes. I'm sorry Mandy for stealing the silver spoon from your tea set when I was four, and for taking your Bridal Barbie when I was eight, and your best pen when I was ten. I'm sorry for stealing your pink elephant from your elephant collection when I was twelve and your new black mascara when I was fifteen. And I'm really sorry for stealing your favourite shirt when I was sixteen." She stops and runs her hand through her messed-up hair.

"And most of all I'm so sorry for stealing your boyfriend and hurting you when I was seventeen. And for running away and leaving you alone. It was a terrible, horrible thing to do. And I've missed you every day for thirteen years." Tears start streaming down her cheeks and she doesn't bother to wipe them away. "And I'm sorry, Tiff," she turns to me, "for stealing things and money from other people because I thought they would make us happy. And I'm sorry, Cass," she turns to Auntie Cass, "for leaving you and hurting you and not letting you know where I was and not even telling you that Tiff was born. And I'm sorry," she says, slumping in a heap on the floor, "for being so stupid and getting hauled off to prison."

All the diners draw in a shocked breath and hold it, not daring to let it go.

"There," she spits into the dining room. "The truth is out. I haven't been away working at all, you see. I've been slammed up in prison for the past three months for doing stupid, stupid things. But do you know?" she smiles. "I'm glad for that. I'm glad I went to prison because going to prison has meant that I'm back home now, with my family, where I belong."

I gasp, because finally our secret is out, and although I'm worried what everyone will say, I know that the truth is best. Secrets and lies cause too much sadness and too much pain. Right then, Mandy slumps down next to Mum. Then she opens her arms wide and folds her friend into a massive hug. They sit there for ages, gently holding each other.

"I've never stopped loving you either," Mandy sniffs. "I've missed you and your crazy ways a million times a day. And I accept your apology. Let's start afresh shall we?"

Mum nods, snuggling herself deeper into Mandy's hug.

"And thanks for remembering my birthday." She wipes Mum's tears away and kisses her cheek.

Chapter 35

I think I have some good news too. . .

I shove Holly into the kitchen and we get busy lighting the candles on Mandy's cake. It's an enormous chocolate one full of cream and raspberries.

"That's my mum's most favourite cake in the whole wide world," smiles Holly, her green eyes lighting up.

"I know," I smile. "My mum remembered."

When we walk back into the bar the whole room bursts into 'Happy Birthday' singing. Mandy's bitter face looks like someone's put a beautiful light behind it and switched her on. I've never seen her look so happy. And Mum too. Me and Holly perch on high bar stools and help ourselves to some of the amazing cake. Mandy and

Mum and are still snuggled up close, talking quietly and unwrapping the present, when Max and Isla rush in.

"Where have you been today?" I ask, cutting them each a slice of cake.

"Well," says Isla, "we both have some amazing news."

Holly and I look at each other and smother a giggle. "You're not getting married are you?" asks Holly.

"No, dummy," says Max, raising his eyebrows. "We're not getting married, no, but I did go and get that dyslexic test thingy done, Tiff, and you're right, I'm not stupid. In fact I have a really high IQ. So I'll be able to be a zoologist after all."

"That's brilliant news, Dr Max," I smile.

"And you, Isla," says Holly, "what's your news?"

"I did it," she squeals. "I finally told my parents about not wanting to go away to school. And that I want to stop playing the violin and take up the flute instead and that I hate pink and everything. It just all came spilling out."

"And?" I say.

"And I don't have to go away to school. I'm staying here. Forever!"

"Brilliant!" Holly and me say at exactly the same time.

"Jinx!" says Holly.

"Jinx to you," I say, and as I look into her emerald eyes, something hits me like a massive, big, lightning flash.

I can't believe I haven't worked it out before. I can't believe no one else has worked it out before. Everything suddenly makes sense. I push my bar stool away and stand in the middle of the room. All eyes are on me. Watching.

"Well," I say, my voice wobbling with nerves, "I think I have some news too." I turn to look at Holly and she looks back at me.

"I can't believe we haven't worked this out before, Holly, but if I'm right, your dad left your mum to be with my mum. Which left both of our mums with a baby, namely you and me. . . and I think that means—"

"That you and me are sisters," whispers Holly.

Chapter 36

There's no place like home...

It's three o'clock and my mum and Mandy still haven't stopped sobbing. And I think me and Holly are still in shock, we just keep on staring at each other and giggling. I truly can't believe that I have a real-live sister in the world and that she's sitting right next to me, eating a second helping of cake. We're holding hands. We're sisters.

I look over at my mum and notice that she's shining again from the inside. Just like in that photo of her and Auntie Cass on their ponies. Right now, she's sitting close to Mandy, munching her cake and sipping champagne, wearing crazy chef clothes, and she's not even bothered. She doesn't care how she looks. There's not a shiny thing or diamond in sight, yet she looks like she's been plugged in to some source of shiny happiness.

And I'm shining too. I can feel happiness streaming out of me like a fountain, filling the room and lighting up my green, green eyes. And now I know for sure that Matilda was wrong and that all the hurts and tight little scars in the world can be melted by love.

So I laugh out loud. My mum has found her friend, and Mandy has found my mum. Max has found his brain, and Isla has found the courage to tell her family what she really wants. As for my sister, Holly? Well, by the way she's hugging me right now, I'm pretty sure she's found her heart. And me? I've found a precious family that I never knew I had and here I am, totally swimming in love.

I click my ruby slippers three times and in my very best American Dorothy accent, I giggle, "There's no place like home, there's no place like home, there's no place like home."

Acknowledgements

Thank you Daniel, for all the love, support, delicious dinners, toasty fires, beautiful garden, house building, enthusiasm and listening ears throughout the entire process of creating *Shine*. Thank you Jane, Tim, Sam, Joe and Ben for your enthusiasm, encouragement and patience and for being so wonderfully shiny yourselves! I'm so proud of you all! Thank you my lovely sister Susie, for celebration champagne and heart-to-hearts and constant sisterly love. Thank you my lovely friend Dawne, for our friendship and your million-times daily emails full of love and support and for being my tip top grown-up reader! Thank you Paul, for always believing in me, always loving me. Thank you all my little readers: Alice, Ruby,

Autumn, Louis, Bryany, Bay and Darcey and anyone else I've forgotten (sorry!) for your helpful feedback. Thank you Dao, Amida, Benita and Claudia for all your love, patience and encouragement with *Shine* whilst on retreat and for lending me your names! Thank you Sophie, Clara, Roseanna and Michelle for all the horsey help. Thank you Sarah Cottle and staff and all the lovely children of Sark School for welcoming me into your world and Kristina, for hot chocolate and Sark gossip.

Thank you a million times over wonderful Eve, my agent, for believing in me and for all your support, care and loveliness. And thank you wonderful Rachel, my editor, for agreeing with Eve and for guiding me so tenderly through the whole process of bringing *Shine* into being. I'm so happy! Thank you Rose, Kate, Tom and Heike, from HarperCollins, for all your hard work and enthusiasm and for diligently working through all the stuff that has to be done before words on a screen become a book on a shelf.

Thank you Adam, for your love, commitment and support in helping me to unwrap my very own inner shine.

I feel so blessed. xxx

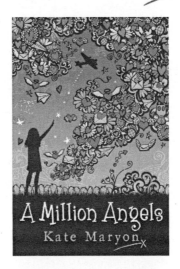

Printed by RR Donnelley at Glasgow, UK